Praise for the Novels of Alison Pace

Through Thick and Thin

"[A] sensitive and knowing exploration of the trickiness—and value—of meaningful relationships." —*Kirkus Reviews*

"Alison Pace's take on single-in-the-city is refreshingly honest and poignant." —*Desert Living Magazine*

"Endearing...craftily portraying the balancing act between work and play, family (be it four-legged or two) and friends, and food and fasting." —*Publishers Weekly*

"A tale of two sisters that charmed me, and even better, introduced me to the wry and artful writing of Alison Pace."
—Elizabeth McKenzie, author of *Stop That Girl*

Pug Hill

"I adored *Pug Hill*...a great example of a single-girl-in-the-city narrator who's not sparkly or ditzy, but neurotic and a little sad...You hope for good things to happen to her, and cheer when they do. Also, I can't remember when I've seen such sensitive and funny writing about dogs."
—Jennifer Weiner, author of *Certain Girls*

"Pace is enjoyable and clever, throwing in sly commentary on our current social scene à la Jane Austen." —*The Miami Herald*

"Smart and witty." —*Library Journal*

"A delightful romp! Alison Pace's dry and breezy wit makes this a delightful, funny read for pugs and humans alike."
—Wilson the Pug with Nancy Levine, authors of *The Tao of Pug*

continued...

city dog

ALISON PACE

BERKLEY BOOKS, NEW YORK

THE BERKLEY PUBLISHING GROUP
Published by the Penguin Group
Penguin Group (USA) Inc.
375 Hudson Street, New York, New York 10014, USA
Penguin Group (Canada), 90 Eglinton Avenue East, Suite 700, Toronto, Ontario M4P 2Y3, Canada
(a division of Pearson Penguin Canada Inc.)
Penguin Books Ltd., 80 Strand, London WC2R 0RL, England
Penguin Group Ireland, 25 St. Stephen's Green, Dublin 2, Ireland (a division of Penguin Books Ltd.)
Penguin Group (Australia), 250 Camberwell Road, Camberwell, Victoria 3124, Australia
(a division of Pearson Australia Group Pty. Ltd.)
Penguin Books India Pvt. Ltd., 11 Community Centre, Panchsheel Park, New Delhi—110 017, India
Penguin Group (NZ), 67 Apollo Drive, Rosedale, North Shore 0632, New Zealand
(a division of Pearson New Zealand Ltd.)
Penguin Books (South Africa) (Pty.) Ltd., 24 Sturdee Avenue, Rosebank, Johannesburg 2196,
South Africa

Penguin Books Ltd., Registered Offices: 80 Strand, London WC2R 0RL, England

This book is an original publication of The Berkley Publishing Group.

Copyright © 2008 by Alison Pace.
Text design by Tiffany Estreicher.

PRINTING HISTORY
Berkley trade paperback edition / September 2008

Library of Congress Cataloging-in-Publication Data

Pace, Alison.
    City dog / Alison Pace.
        p.   cm.
    ISBN 978-0-425-22143-3
    1. Women authors—Fiction.   2. Television programs—Fiction.   3. New York (N.Y.)—
Fiction.   [1. Dogs—Training—Fiction.]   I. Title.
    PS3566.A24C58 2008
    813'.54—dc22

                                                                2008014243

PRINTED IN THE UNITED STATES OF AMERICA

10   9   8   7   6   5   4   3   2   1

For Joanna
(who got the party, so to speak, started)

acknowledgments

As always, many thanks to my editor, Susan Allison, to my agent, Joe Veltre, and to all the great people at Berkley Books, especially Leslie Gelbman, Rita Frangie (she of all the fantastic covers), Megan Swartz, and Danielle Stockley.

For help in matters of geographical research, Westie acquisition, veterinarian queries, and "things about TV," much appreciation goes to Anthony Roth Costanzo, Mary Schafer, Nancy Simpkins, Dr. Carrie Osterman, and Robin Epstein. Cheers to Jane Pace for wading through the early drafts, and thanks to Elinor Lipman for a very encouraging read at the darkest hour.

Ongoing love and thanks go out to my family and friends, who are all very good at understanding when I must embrace my inner recluse.

And last, but certainly not least, much love and a lifetime supply of cheese to Carlie, really excellent muse, even better best friend.

I can hear the voice inside my head.
—Dixie Chicks

I

(amy)

I Ran, I Ran So Far Away

I was divorced," he says.

He tilts his head as he says it, so that one of his eyes is hidden behind the candlestick that sits between us. I look across the table: I see one eye, one candlestick, and the hint of a grin that's not even the slightest bit sheepish. I think his grin should be at least slightly sheepish.

For now though, I don't have time to think about the intricacies of his expression. I'm too busy thinking about what he just said. *I was divorced.* I'm not thinking about the fact that I should have known this already, that "I was divorced" should have perhaps made an appearance in one of our earlier conversations. I'm thinking about the verb. *Was*, the past tense of *be*. I'm jealous of the verb. Yes, I do have a fleeting interest in the fact that his divorce somehow managed to slip his mind even when this very topic came up, several conversations ago. But mostly, I'm jealous of the word *was*.

I was married. Past tense, there it is, I am in fact quite good at using it. But I *am* divorced. And I've never, or at least not in the three years since I *have been* divorced, had it slip my mind.

As we, the man who was divorced and I, get up from the table and leave the restaurant, as we walk toward my street, I feel somehow relieved. I think it's a good thing that he said that. Not because it brings us closer because we're both divorced (even though he *was* and I *am*) but because he didn't tell me until now, until well after the time when he really already should have. This, I think, can be the thing he did wrong. This can be the reason I won't feel at all inclined to go out with him again. I had an open mind and gave it a chance and look, he wasn't a straight-up guy and didn't tell me about his divorce even though I'd told him about mine. And also, he used a verb that I couldn't comprehend.

We're standing on the sidewalk in front of my building now, and I want him to start walking in any direction. Any direction he chooses will take him away from me. I take out my keys. I wonder if there's a certain way to hold my keys that could wordlessly say, *When I turn this key in the door, I only mean it for me. I don't mean it for you. You, over there, you're not getting invited up.*

I explain that I'm tired, that I've got an early meeting in the morning. The first part is true. The second part is a lie.

"Okay then," he says, and I smile, not warmly. "Amy," he continues, leaning in a bit as he says it, and I inadvertently clench my teeth, "I had a really nice time tonight."

"I did, too," I say, another lie. He smiles back at me, and I think about how many things would have to be different in order for what I just said to be true. He turns and begins walking west, and I turn to put my key in the door.

I'm here, turning a key in the door of a hot-pink brick building on East Fifth Street, for a lot of reasons. Either the first or last of those reasons is that I left my husband. Or maybe it's because I married him. It's hard for me to say for sure. I'm not sure where it all started exactly, and a lot of the time I think maybe it's because of the dream.

For as far back as I can remember I have had the same recurring dream: I've moved into a very big house and I don't have any furniture. In the dream, there is no discernible happiness at the vastness of my house; I am not heard exclaiming, "This is really excellent, I have a lovely, large home." There's just a tremendous amount of anxiety, much more than seems appropriate, over the fact that I don't have enough things to fill the rooms upon rooms. There are indeed rooms upon rooms; doors just keep opening and opening to wide-open, architecturally intricate spaces. Sometimes the spaces are round.

I met Jonathan when I was twenty-four—Jonathan, who *was* my husband, Jonathan, who is my ex. We met in June. I remember that it was under a tent in Bryant Park behind the New York Public Library. I remember that it was at a party where everyone was wearing Lilly Pulitzer, but I can no longer remember why everyone was dressed that way. I'd only just arrived in New York and was toiling away, somewhat reluctantly, in the events department of an enormous public relations firm. I was a young, bright-eyed, transplanted Coloradoan standing at a party with a clipboard.

Jonathan had walked over to my station and he'd asked me, "Do you have the name Jonathan Dodge on that there clipboard?" I remember feeling certain, as I told him that I did in fact have his name on my clipboard, that he'd known it was there all along. He asked me what I did. I imagined he meant when I wasn't with my clipboard, and even though it wasn't exactly the truth, I told him I was a writer.

And then I don't remember much of what else came before he told me, "I'm an antiques dealer."

"Furniture," he said next, its own solitary sentence.

And then, also separately, also standing alone, "Decorative objects."

It made so much sense. It seemed to my twenty-four-year-old self like the perfect, fated match. I remember thinking that maybe my dreams had been looking for Jonathan all my life. I remember thinking that it, all of it, just had to be symbolic. Beautifully, simply, and perfectly symbolic. I was twenty-five when Jonathan and I got married. We moved into Jonathan's townhouse on Ninety-third Street just off Madison Avenue. The house, and all the furniture in it, had been in Jonathan's family for generations. I started working soon after in the library of Dodge's, his family's antiques gallery. I thought it surely possible that being surrounded by books could be, in its way, preparation for one day writing them. My entire life had been completely furnished in one great swoop. It wasn't until years later that it occurred to me that I hadn't picked out very many of the things in it.

I was the first person I knew in New York to get married. I had no idea then that I'd be the first person I knew to be divorced. I had no idea then that I'd be the person packing up all of her belongings (of which it turned out there were not very many) and getting, quite literally, the hell out of Dodge. I was so sure when I met Jonathan that I had found absolutely everything I'd been looking for. I don't think that anymore.

Three flights of stairs now behind me, I put another

key into another lock. I can hear Carlie inside, jumping on and/or throwing herself against the door. I smile. In spite of anything, in spite of everything, she always makes me smile.

"Hi," I say, opening the door. "Well, hello!"

2

(carlie)

I Don't Want to Work, I Just Want to Bang on the Drum All Day

This is a book about me!

My name is Carlie. I am a three-and-a-half-year-old West Highland White Terrier, which means that I am a small, game, hardy, and well-balanced-looking terrier. It means that I am the most genial of all the terriers, that I was originally bred for the hunting of both rodents and vermin, and that my ancestors hail from Scotland.

Amy has just returned from being on the other side of the door. We have had our greeting at the door in which Amy smiles at the very sight of me and says in her very nice and very happy voice, "Hello!" And I have responded, in kind, "Hello!" but she has not heard me. Amy is not the best listener. I have found that remarkably few people are any good at listening, but sometimes I wonder if maybe Amy is especially bad.

Amy and I have gone out for the last walk of the day, the one that is usually an hour or two before Amy tells me she has "zee bone for zee bed," and then tells me that "another day has come to an end," in the soft voice, the voice that sounds a little bit like singing and makes me want to wag my tail very fast and sleep with my head right up on the pillow. The last walk of the day is always very quick. There is no turning down Second Avenue and walking to Fourth Street and then back up to the Cooper Square street, in the shape of a square, like there is at other times of the day. At this time of night we do not make the shape of a square. It is only straight, there and back, all of it on Fifth Street, all of it business. We are back already, and I have been given a snack treat, which is different from "zee bone for zee bed" in that it is earlier, and also, not announced.

Amy has gone to look at the white rectangle shape that flips open and glows. A lot of the time she pokes at it, and it alternately clicks and beeps and falls silent. She can stare at it mesmerized for hours, even when I try to talk, even when I give my quick *chomp-chomp*, which translates quite literally to "Stop staring at the white rectangle shape and pay attention to me!" Attention, so you know, is very high on the list of my priorities. Yes. If you watch the Westminster Dog Show at Madison

Square Garden on the television when it is the Westie's turn, you will hear the announcer say, "The Westie will not be ignored!" The announcer speaks the truth. And then, after some blah blah blah, as the Westie begins to run down the length of the show ring, the announcer will describe her as "possessed of no small amount of self-esteem." They say this exact thing, year after year, because it is true. Though that is not to say that simply repeating things year after year will make it so that they are true, because it does not.

Where was I? Right, Amy is staring at the white rectangle shape and could be for a while, so I've got some time, and I wanted to let you know, in case you were wondering, that this is a book about me.

Yes, it is a book about Amy. And it is a book about Amy and Jonathan, or at least about the end of them. It is about Robert Maguire sometimes, and Renee and Lara, and Nick and Bonnie, and also someone we do not like called Erin. But you have not met any of those people yet, seeing as how it is still very early in the story. So let us forget about all the other people for now, or at least try really hard to. I have learned that people can have a hard time forgetting about things. I have also learned that people have a way of becoming quite easily confused.

I know that sometimes Amy gets confused. I know that sometimes Amy does not know where to start her story. I am here to tell you that it is not that confusing.

The story started when Amy and Jonathan drove to Cape May, New Jersey, and got me. Right before that there had been a number of years that Amy will refer to sometimes as "The Baby Debates," and at other times she will refer to them as "The End." What happened is that during The Baby Debates, Jonathan told Amy, who wanted a baby, that he wanted one, too, just not right yet. And then after saying that for a few years, he said he did not—want a baby, that is. I think that is when the period of time changed in Amy's mind from The Baby Debates to The End. Also, I think that must be how I know that just because you say something year after year, it does not mean it is true.

And so Amy and Jonathan drove to Cape May, New Jersey, which is where I come from, and they got me. *Instead* is a word I believe may have been used. But that is not something I like to think about.

I liked the first neighborhood I lived in in New York City, and I very much liked the Central Park that was right at the end of our block. It was very big, much bigger than the park we go to now. But we didn't stay there very long, and then I wasn't with Amy and Jonathan anymore, then I was just with Amy. I do not ever remember feeling bad about that, and I do not know for sure what happened to Jonathan. I do not know for certain where he went. I think that he stayed there, in the house I lived in when I was young, the one that had stairs on the same side of the door as all the furniture. There was a lot of furniture there; there was a Chippendale sofa in particular, upon which I was not allowed. For some reason my being on that sofa often resulted in Jonathan referring to me not as Carlie (as I understandably prefer to be called) but as "the dog."

"Amy," he would say, "can you get *the dog* off the Chippendale sofa." And he did so in a way that I felt lacked a certain respect, revealed perhaps a less-than-generous spirit.

Soon after I met him, Jonathan faded out. It was a slow fade, but even so, I never felt I knew him well. Never once did I sense him to be an enduring presence in my life, even during my uptown puppyhood. To be perfectly honest, at this point I do not wish to remember him.

And then we moved here, to Fifth Street. It is in a place called the East Village and Amy said it was as far away as she could get from the Upper East Side, which is where we lived before. This does not make very much sense to me, because even I can think of places farther.

We came to Fifth Street and spent our mornings in a park that was smaller and called Tompkins Square Park, where I made friends but Amy did not. Amy did not spend very much time at all talking to even one of the very many people who are always there, gathered in small pairs, and bigger clusters, and even bigger groups. Instead of talking, as so many of the other people seem so keen to do, Amy spent a lot of time thinking about the novel she wanted to write. When she talked to me about it, she would say how she wanted it to be a Great American Novel. But she did not write a novel, Great American or otherwise.

She wrote a book about me.

Run, Carlie, Run!: The Adventures of Carlie.

Though to be technically correct, *Run, Carlie, Run!: The Adventures of Carlie* is actually a book about the adventures of me and Robert Maguire, the Scottish explorer who accompanies me on my adventures. It began as something that Amy worked on when she was not writing her Great American Novel, her great, important, literary tome.

Three years later, said tome has not been worked on very much at all. But *Run, Carlie, Run!: The Adventures of Carlie*—the story of how I traveled to Scotland and lingered too long on the banks of Loch Ness and almost met my demise at the snout of the Loch Ness Monster until Robert Maguire alerted me to danger by shouting (I bet you can guess), "Run, Carlie, run!"—has been worked on quite a lot. Soon after its completion, *Run, Carlie, Run!* had someone important called a literary agent, it was sold to a very big publishing house, and I heard "an illustrator was attached," which means there was a person who drew pictures of me to match the words Amy wrote about me. And then the book was published and sent out into the world, where it was met with the greatest acclaim. *Run, Carlie, Run!: The Adventures of Carlie* was followed up quickly by *Run, Carlie, Run!: Carlie in Paris* and then *Run, Carlie, Run!: Carlie in the Congo*. There was a precarious perch atop La Tour Eiffel; there was a rogue crocodile in the Congo. Robert Maguire and I averted them all.

Each of the three books about me has been on a bestseller list at one time or another. I have been translated into twenty-seven languages. I have received numerous accolades, and, once, an award. I have heard it said that there is not a child under the age of ten who does not know the name Carlie. There are lunchboxes, notebooks, figurines made in my likeness, and as of just recently, Fruit Roll-Ups bearing my name.

I am not altogether sure how happy any of this makes Amy, not when she really thinks about it. I heard her say once that she was not sure this is what she wanted to be remembered for, if a picture book about her dog (I did not appreciate the leaving out of my name) was what her life's work was supposed to be. And then I got confused or something else caught my attention, probably the latter. I think there was a bird on the windowsill.

If you ask me, and you might as well, I think she takes it all too seriously. I have things that I work on, that I put a lot of care and time and energy into. For example, I am systematically defringing the Oriental rug in the living room. It is long work, and it is tiring work, and also to avoid detection, it is work I must go about very slowly, under the cloak of darkness, or at least when I am here alone with only the Dixie Chicks for company. Who knows when I will finish? But I do not get all dramatic about it and call it my life's work. No, I prefer to think of it as my current project.

I see that Amy has moved away from the white rectangle shape and has made her way into the kitchen. She takes one of the boxes from the cupboard. Oh, look, it is the tall white one. It is a truth that I feel a great love for all boxes that are removed from the cupboard, but I especially love the tall white box with the large blue writing. I do not know what the writing says, but I know what is inside this particular box. The salt cracker. Now, like magic, Amy has the salt cracker in her hand.

I am sorry, but I have to go.

3

(amy)

They Don't Write 'Em Like That Anymore

I turn on my laptop. I open up the blank Word document that I have gone so far as to title *Swim, Carlie, Swim!* and I stare at the empty page. I look down at Carlie. Carlie is wearing a turquoise bandana. Earlier, I had taken it out of the top drawer of the dresser and tied it in a jaunty manner around Carlie's neck. My hope had been that the turquoise color would surely put me in mind of water, or at least of something nautical. I felt that the bandana itself, regardless of its color—even if it were red, yellow, green—might lend a certain cowboy-like feel, a pioneer spirit to the room.

Carlie looks up at me from her current resting place, the blue-and-white mattress-ticking dog bed I have placed just to the left of my desk.

"Swim, Carlie, swim!" I read out loud to her in the hope that it will help. Her eyes dart off to the side. Her attention is fleeting at best; I need to come up with something more exciting in order to keep it. I know this. But I don't have anything else. The only things I have (in addition to an ongoing case of writer's block, that is) are the words *Swim, Carlie, Swim* and an exclamation point. Though the exclamation point is always there, so I can hardly count it as a new creative achievement. Since I can't read words I don't yet have, I remain silent, looking down at Carlie with the hope that just the sight of her will provide inspiration. Often it does, but no such luck today. Carlie puts her head back down, curls herself up against the edge of her dog bed, and lets out a world-weary sigh. It does seem that her sigh might have been made for the express purpose of highlighting the futility of my endeavors. I am, nonetheless, compelled to try again. "Swim, Carlie, swim!" No reaction. None at all.

I have sat down at my desk, again, to write *Swim, Carlie, Swim!: Carlie on the Snake River*. As described to my agent, and in turn to my editor, this book will take Carlie and Robert Maguire on a white-water rafting expedition on the fabled Snake River, the roughest part of it in wildest Wyoming (so clearly you can see why a pioneer spirit could indeed come in handy). That is, of course, if I ever actually write it. I try to get myself into the right frame of mind. I remind myself that I have in fact done this all before. Carlie and her trusty compan-ion, Robert Maguire, have already traveled to Scotland and courted grave danger on the banks of Loch Ness; they've gone to Paris and climbed to the top of the Eiffel Tower. They have eluded all types of danger both floral and faunal in the Congo. When I think of it all now, I have no idea how it happened.

I have no idea how I wrote it. It was never something I set out purposely to do. And now, faced with the task of doing it again, I'm not altogether sure I'll be able to recapture how it all started.

Upon the occasion of my divorce, I had, as they say, checked out. I left my husband and while I was at it, I left the things that were a part of my life with him. The house, the furniture, and the majority of the friends. Most of the friends I had shared with my husband had quickly begun to feel like friends from another time. They became, in their literal and figurative distance, no longer real to me, like science fiction time-warp people. And it was so much easier for me to let them go. There was in fact only one friend I kept—Lara—and truthfully, the times are many that I wish I hadn't.

I moved here, to the East Village, because I wanted to get far away, but I didn't want to leave New York. I'd come to New York to be a writer and I'd spent all this time here and I hadn't written anything. I thought mov-ing to the East Village was a bold move, a great step, a bit pioneering in spirit itself if you will. Now, though it is still several physical and metaphorical miles away from the Carnegie Hill townhouse where I spent eight years of my life, sometimes I think it's not quite as far away as I'd intended.

Upon the occasion of my checking out and moving to the East Village, I also saw a psychologist. This was not actually my idea, but rather the idea of my mother, newly energized and vigilant in her newfound role as parent of a single child.

"Amy," she told me, "I feel very strongly that, now of all times, you should see someone." As a professor of sociology, my mother has always had a reverence for the field of psychology, or maybe it's just something that's been ingrained in her the way New Yorkers, to me at least, seem to have an affinity for therapy. Both of my parents are born-and-bred New Yorkers, transplanted to Colorado by way of academia (the University of Colorado at Boulder, to be exact) in the same way I am a born-and-bred Coloradoan, transplanted to New York City by way of I don't know what anymore, my misplaced literary ambitions, some belief I've always had that in order to be a writer, you had to be in New York.

So right, the psychologist. I thought seeing her might actually help me unearth material for the novel I was sure I was meant to write, the novel I felt I needed to get away from everyone and everything in order to write, my

Great American Novel, my modern-day *Great Gatsby*, set perhaps on Madison Avenue and Ninety-third Street. The psychologist's name was Beryl, but you don't need to commit her name to memory because she didn't last. Beryl had wanted to talk mostly about how I didn't have very many friends at this "transitional stage" of my life.

"Carlie is my friend," I explained.

"Carlie is not enough," I was told.

I threw in Lara for good measure and even left out the part that I no longer liked her.

This did not deter Beryl from wondering aloud if perhaps I was deeply depressed. I assured her that I wasn't. I explained that all the time I spent alone had to do with the fact that I was just the type of person who enjoyed spending time alone, and that the *alone* wasn't even alone in the true sense of the word, because of Carlie. I explained how I saw this as an overall good thing, seeing as what I really wanted to do with my life was to be a writer and as far as I could tell, if what a person wanted was to be a writer, it was an occupational imperative to spend a good deal of time very much alone. And then I had to take a very deep breath because it was, after all, a very long sentence. Beryl nodded at me.

"Have you ever tried to have a social life while writing a novel?" I asked her. "I'm not so sure the two are possible," I added, because I'm really not.

"But, Amy," Beryl said to me next, "correct me if I'm

wrong, but as far as I've been made aware, you aren't actually writing a novel."

I told her I felt that was beside the point. She wondered, a bit too predictably, in my mind, how that made me feel.

"I don't know," I said.

"Have you considered," she asked me, "the possibility of walking depression? It's like walking pneumonia." She went on to explain that people could actually walk around, happy, for years even, without actually ever knowing that anything at all was the matter.

"It's amazing," she told me. "People can talk themselves into anything."

In this order, I stopped seeing Beryl (much to the chagrin of my mother), spent what could easily be classified as a tremendous amount of time alone with Carlie, and found it quite difficult to write about anyone in my novel other than my protagonist. Somewhere along the way I started contemplating adventures Carlie might have were she to travel the world with a dashing Scottish explorer. I like to believe there is a way of looking at it all so that it seems logical and linear. And eventually, in a frame of mind that I at least would call somewhat refreshed, I resurfaced.

And when I resurfaced, I did not emerge as the female answer to the Jonathans Lethem, Franzen, and Safran

Foer. No. I returned as the author of *Run, Carlie, Run!: The Adventures of Carlie*. It had not been my plan.

The sound of the ringing phone brings me back to the present again, to my desk again, situated in front of my laptop, staring at the blank white page.

"Hello," I say.

"Amy? It's Renee Van."

Renee Van, my agent. I pause for a moment before saying anything. I always do. I think I might be waiting for her to finish her last name. I always feel like there should be more to it, as if she's about to say, "Amy, it's Renee Vandermeer," or Van der Veyden or Van Tropp. Van something. And I think also, every time, I'm waiting for her to tell me that it's all been a joke, to tell me that the Carlie books weren't as successful as I had been led to believe. That no one actually does so well with a children's book about a wandering Westie and the dashing Scottish explorer who keeps her company.

I wait for her to say, "It was fun, right? And at times, funny, too? But it didn't actually happen, none of it did." And if that happened, if it turned out that the *Run, Carlie, Run!* books were not in fact a thrice-published success story, if it turned out that none of it had happened after all, I'm not sure I would look upon that as a completely bad thing. While I'm proud of the Carlie books, and grateful for the success, if it turned out that none of it had happened, I might welcome the time, the freedom, the psychic space in which to do something else, something different, something more along the lines of what I was really meant to do. Because, at the risk of repeating myself, I'm not altogether certain it's this.

"Hi, Renee," I say once I'm sure that longer last names and revelations about the last three years are not forthcoming.

"Amy!" She is talking louder and quicker than even her usual loud and quick. "I trust you're well and so I'm going to just jump right to it, because it is *outstanding*. I've just gotten off the phone with the people at DTV. Get ready. Are you ready? Are you sitting down? Because you should be sitting down for this!"

"I'm sitting," I tell her.

"Okay, this is fantastic. They've offered us a show! A show on DTV! Carlie will host!"

"DTV?" I ask.

"Yes! DTV!" Renee exclaims, though that in itself doesn't necessarily mean it's exciting. Renee does tend toward the exclamation. "You know," she continues, "it's the cable channel? It's been called 'Lifetime for Dogs'? Amy, you of all people should know about DTV." She adds on a good-natured chuckle, but still, if I had to say, I'd say that last part was a little condescending.

"No, I know," I say defensively, even though the likelihood could have been high that I didn't. For someone who doesn't like to go out much, I don't watch very much TV either.

"Right," Renee continues, "so, like I said, they've offered us a show on TV. Amy, this is great. I mean, *everyone* wants to be on TV."

"Right," I say back, because, sure, I imagine she could very well be right. I imagine there must be so many people out there in the world who want to be on television. I'd just never before considered that Carlie might be one of them. But maybe everyone does want to be on TV, maybe everyone actually wants to be famous. I think of the Carlie lunchboxes, the Carlie action figures, the fact that just last week, Carlie was stopped on the street.

"And you would co-host," Renee tells me next, before I can finish my thoughts.

"I would co-host?" I ask, and as I repeat Renee's words, I think, yes, a little bit about being on TV, but more about the fact that being a co-host could mean gainful employment, gainful employment that had nothing at all to do with sitting down, day after day, and staring at a blank and, in my mind, unforgiving computer screen. It could be, I think, a most welcome distraction from the difficulty that is tentatively titled *Swim, Carlie, Swim!* Granted, all the Carlie books were in themselves a distraction from the novel I couldn't seem to write. But regardless, the wheels have begun turning. Technically, I could still "work" on *Swim, Carlie, Swim!*, still think about it, but this way, I'll be required to think about something else, too. Writing is hard. Distractions are important. This, I think, could be just the distraction I need.

"Yes, it's going to be a weekly show featuring you and Carlie," Renee explains. "I mean, ideally it would be better if it could have been Carlie and Robert Maguire, but since he doesn't exist, they want to go with you."

I try simultaneously not to take that personally and also to remember that I have recently made a (so far unmaintainable) pact with myself to stop lamenting the fact that Robert Maguire does not actually exist. I do sometimes wish that he did. Maybe it's slightly more than sometimes. I know that to some people it might seem strange that I spend a fair amount of time wishing that the fictional Scottish explorer I invented to travel the world with my dog was real. To those people, I say this: Before you judge, try dating in New York in your thirties for a while. You, too, might spend a bit more time than could be considered appropriate contemplating how much nicer everything would be for you if your fictional Scottish explorer actually existed.

"Okay," I say to Renee because of course I can understand the television people's interest in Robert Maguire.

"Okay!" Renee says, all energy, all excitement, all forward motion.

"Okay!" I say back, though to exactly what at this point

I don't know. Change is good, I remind myself. Not writing anything day after day is bad.

"Obviously the *Run, Carlie, Run!* books will be the jumping-off point," Renee continues.

"Obviously," I say. Renee's enthusiasm can be catching. It occurs to me that though the fictional Carlie and Robert Maguire have been to Paris, I never have. I certainly haven't been to the Congo, or even to Scotland. I think for that moment how nice it might be to get out of New York for a while. All the *Run, Carlie, Run!* books take place outside New York. Maybe things start with leaving New York.

"You know," I say, "it might be really nice to travel."

"Right, that's great, Amy," Renee says and I hear the slight note of hesitation in her voice. "But this show is going to take place in New York." Somewhere, in a parallel universe where CDs and MP3s have yet to be invented, a needle is being scratched across a record.

"*Run, Carlie, Run!: Carlie in New York?*" I ask, and as soon as I've said it out loud, I don't like the sound of it. It's not the sound I was hoping for.

"Not exactly. The show is going to be called *Things to Do in the City with Your Dog*. It's going to be about how great New York is, and how many ways there are to enjoy it with your dog! Very I heart my dog. Very I heart New York."

Only, I think, *I don't heart New York.* Everyone loves

New York, but the thing is, I don't think I do anymore. I'm not altogether certain if that's because New York has been the backdrop for my misdirected writing career, or before that, the scene of my mistaken marriage. Maybe it's simply because it's the current setting of my writer's block. I'm not able to say for sure.

"Do you want to talk about the money?" Renee asks. Renee, I imagine, would like to talk about the money. I would prefer to be the type of person who could say something along the lines of, "I don't want to talk about money because it gets in the way of my art." But as my gaze falls on the computer screen in front of me, I am reminded that my art right now is a blank white page. There is not only the matter of the writer's block. There is not only the matter of the novel I may never write. There is the matter of the phone call I made to Jonathan when *Run, Carlie, Run!: The Adventures of Carlie* hit that first bestseller list, the one in which I told him I no longer needed or wanted alimony. At present, I am still the type of person who needs to talk about the money.

"I do," I tell her. "But let me just think on it for a minute first. I'll call you back."

"All right, all right," she says quickly, just like it's one chirpy multisyllabic word. *Allrightallright*. "Think about it, absolutely, think about it. You have to do what's best for you. But Amy, this could really be something." *Could be*, I repeat to myself. Everything could be something.

"I think you'd be crazy to let it go," Renee concludes. "Why don't you think about it? Think about it and then call me back and say, 'Renee, yes!'"

"Okay," I say and then I hang up quickly.

I stare at the phone in its receiver and then I turn and stare at the blank computer screen. I stare at it for a while longer.

And then I pick up the phone.

4

(amy)

If You Were Here,
You Would Believe

Just a minute," I say through the intercom, in response to Renee's buzz. Renee has just arrived to take Carlie, and me, via car service no less, to the production studio where *Things to Do in the City with Your Dog* will be filmed. The first day of our cable television lives. I am pleased that Carlie and I will be traveling by car service. If we weren't, we'd be journeying by subway, with Carlie in her travel bag, and Carlie seems to have more than a passing dislike of her travel bag. I imagine this is my fault. I didn't introduce her to the travel bag when she was a young, comparatively more moldable pup. I had no way of knowing then that her life wouldn't always be one of riding in cars whenever transport was necessary. I had no way of knowing that her life wouldn't always be lived within the lofty confines of Carnegie Hill.

As I slide Carlie's harness over her head, clasp it shut, and hook her leash on, I want to be only positive, and I want to think only of the good things. A good attitude, they say it can go such a long way. This television show could be exactly the distraction—or let's not even call it a distraction, let's not paint it with that brush, let's call it a *supplement*—I need in order to really get going on *Swim, Carlie, Swim!* And who knows, maybe even on the novel. And of course, there are bills to pay. There are always bills to pay in New York City, to say nothing of New York City rent.

"Ready?" I say to Carlie, collecting my keys and my bag and heading in the direction of the door. Carlie looks up at me and suddenly, I am struck by the thought that maybe her harness, a utilitarian red mesh Puppia number, isn't the right look for her debut day. Quickly, I grab one of Carlie's collars, the brightly colored one with all the different blocks of stripes and patterns, hand-stitched in Guatemala. As Carlie swans around me, I switch from harness to collar hastily. *Much better,* I think. As I admire the new, improved collar, I realize that I have given almost as much thought to Carlie's outfit as I have to my own. And for me, I gave a bit of thought to my outfit. I look down at my black knee-length skirt and black T-shirt, run a hand over my slightly frizzed, pony-tailed hair, and consider that perhaps I should have given more. I stand up, attach Carlie's new, snazzier leash, and we head together down all the stairs and out onto the street, where Renee awaits with our chariot, or at least, our town car.

"Amy, hi!" Renee says as we slide into the seat beside her. "Carlie looks great."

"Thanks," I say, and try to think that was just a compliment on Carlie's hand-stitched Guatemalan collar, and not anything else. I do not entirely succeed.

"It's good to see you," Renee says next.

"It's good to see you, too," I say, and for the most part, it is. Sometimes I think of Renee as my friend. Though also, it should be noted, sometimes I don't.

As we settle in and head off, the driver cracks the window and Carlie sidles right up next to it in order to best feel the wind in her hair. Carlie enjoys the wind in her hair. The three of us are silent as we snake through the streets of the East Village, heading over to the FDR Drive, which will lead us to the Fifty-ninth Street Bridge, and over it to Long Island City and the studio where DTV films its shows. Long Island City. Queens. I never pictured television studios as being over the bridge in Queens, but then I actually don't know if I've ever pictured them at all.

As we approach the FDR Drive and the East River appears ahead of us, I can see a person kayaking in the choppy water in the distance. I wonder why anyone in their right mind would want to kayak in such dirty water, and then surprisingly, not surprisingly, I don't even know anymore, I find myself wondering about the latest Carlie book. I wonder if *Swim, Carlie, Swim!: Carlie on the Snake River* would work better if Carlie and Robert Maguire were perhaps in a kayak as opposed to a white-water raft? I picture Robert Maguire, perched in his perfection at the edge of a kayak, calling out, "Swim, Carlie, swim!" deliverer of catchphrase, of punch line, and arbiter of safety.

"Amy?" I hear, and I can feel Renee leaning over from her seat and into my space.

"Yes," I say quickly, snapping back to attention.

"Victoria called," she says, looking over at me with wide, concerned eyes, "about the manuscript." I nod. I wonder how long she's been waiting so that enough time has passed so that it didn't seem like she was jumping right into the topic. I nod again.

"Uh-huh," I say. What else can I say? Victoria is the editor for the *Run, Carlie, Run!* series. I'd like to be able to say that it's not necessary to commit her name to memory either. There is the wish that maybe she won't last, either. Though that should not in any way be taken as an indication that Victoria is not a nice person. She is in fact quite pleasant. It's just that the situation, the situation with the latest Carlie book, has steadily been becoming more and more unpleasant.

"I would rather not talk about it today," I say after a while, the emphasis on *today*, evoking the importance of and highlighting my dedication to the new television venture.

Renee reaches over and puts several fingertips on my arm, just under my elbow. It is a gesture that is to me neither soothing nor understanding; it is a gesture that says, *Editors are anxious, illustrators are waiting, plans have been made, deadlines have been missed.* I don't say anything.

"Okay," Renee says next, thankfully not going the way of *but, really, Amy, we need to talk about the manuscript,* because it could in fact have gone that way. "Let's talk about something else."

I find myself nodding purposelessly and smiling a bit benignly, because honestly I can't think of anything else to say.

"What's new with you?" Renee asks. Her hand is once again reaching out to touch my arm but I feel it's much less of a loaded gesture this time. "Anything to report? Any dates?" she asks, transitioning almost seamlessly from agent back to friendlike agent.

"I'm sorry?" I say even though I heard her perfectly.

"Any dates lately?" she repeats, more slowly this time.

"Right," I say, and I think to myself, *any dates.* I think of how much I have come to dislike that question. "Um, no," I say, instead of the more factually accurate, "Yes, and he was divorced but I took issue with his timing, along with his verb preference."

Renee nods at me in a way that is at once understanding and knowing. I try to just nod back and be done with it. I try my best not to think too much about it, but I'm sure she is thinking, *Yes, yes, of course, what with Robert Maguire and all.* I imagine Renee is thinking that I have neither dates nor updates because I'm too preoccupied with Robert Maguire, or with the *idea* of him, whatever you want to call it. I wonder if she's thinking that I'll never find anyone in my post-Jonathan life because I am too hung up on Robert Maguire.

I turn and look out the window. I don't want to talk to Renee about Robert Maguire. Mostly, I wish Renee didn't know anything about my feelings for Robert Maguire. It was, coincidentally, my editor, Victoria, who first filled her in.

"No wonder Amy is single," Victoria had said. "I would be single too if I spent as much time as she must with an image of Robert Maguire in my head."

"It's nothing," I'd lied when Renee had relayed this information to me. "It's not like that at all."

And even though it hadn't really had anything at all to do with her, Renee had reached out and had said to me, "I understand. I'm single in this city, too."

I don't know if Renee really does understand, or if more likely, my editor and agent both think I'm off my rocker and simply refrain from saying so.

I stare out the window, trying to be sure I won't have

to meet Renee's gaze and wonder if what it really says is, *Amy, it's a problem with Robert Maguire*. Because, yes, it is a problem with Robert Maguire. I never meant it to be. I never planned it this way, not that I planned any of it. But for the record, it's not that I in fact actually, viscerally, *want* the fictional character I invented. I don't think it's exactly that. I think I'd just like someone who is very much like him. Because he's smart, and adventurous of spirit, because I imagine he has a big heart, and because he loves my dog, because he understands my dog, and because I've come to believe he understands me. Is it so much to ask? Is it so necessary to believe that he doesn't exist?

We continue without further conversation over the Fifty-ninth Street Bridge and into the edge of Queens to Long Island City. It isn't very long at all that we have to sit in the slightly stifled, slightly awkward, slightly Robert Maguire–infused silence before we pull up outside the studio building. As the three of us disembark from the back of the town car and make our way to the entrance, I notice that Carlie is not stopping to sniff every conceivable surface. Rather, she is walking jauntily, proudly even, right up to the doors.

5

(amy)

The Sun Always Shines on TV

The three of us walk together into the lobby of the studio building. The first thing I notice is the height. The lobby stretches skyward, double height, maybe triple, and even though I can see the ceiling, it makes me think of wide-open spaces. As the years pass, my spaces have been getting smaller and smaller. Here, in this lobby, I imagine I can see that trend reversing. I feel for a moment that if I looked closely enough, I'd be able to see mountains. If I stepped outside and breathed deeply enough, the air would turn out to be free of both humidity and smog.

"We're headed up to the third floor," Renee says. Even as I watch her gesture across the lobby toward the bank of elevators, it doesn't seem possible that there could be anything higher. Even as we enter the elevator and ride up, that feeling stays with me.

As the elevator opens on three, as one impression leaves and another one appears in front of me, I notice the disarray. There is equipment almost everywhere; I have no idea what any of it is for. The wires alone seem omnipresent. There are large boards and wooden structures reclining against walls. And the people, there seem to be quite a lot of them, too. Everyone is very casually dressed. There's a hum in the air, and I feel like I'm in an unsettling dream, one taking place in an electric, tricked-out college dorm. It's a dorm at a city school, there is nothing ivy-covered or bucolic about it. I feel even more out of sorts than usual. I feel it would have been so much nicer to stay downstairs in the lobby.

Though I can't imagine when she's been here before— probably because I've never been very good at wrapping my head around the fact that Renee does have clients other than me—Renee seems to know exactly where she's going. So does Carlie, for that matter: she seems filled up with a great sense of purpose. As we walk down the long, cluttered hallway, I'm following my agent and my dog.

Renee slows down, comes to my side and grabs my elbow. Subsequently, I am steered into a large office. There are two people inside. Seated at a large, cluttered desk is a young woman—younger than me. She has fair skin and pretty brown hair, it's very shiny; I think of a mink. She has it pulled back off her face in a very high ponytail tied up in a white bow. Her eyes are far away from each other, wide set and wide open, and her smile is enthusiastic, slightly openmouthed, very toothy, and, it occurs to me, possibly deranged. She stands up as we enter. Her skirt is black, spandex and short. She is clutching a clipboard firmly against her chest, and I have the impression that at any moment she will burst forth into a run, or perhaps a cheer.

Standing to the left of the desk and slightly behind it is a more-than-slightly-overweight man with a large mustard-colored (if not actually mustard) stain on his striped and untucked shirt. He looks unbalanced, as if at any moment he might tip over. It's as if all his energy has been stolen from him, sucked away from his side of the desk. It's very sunny in here, and I feel for a moment woozy, as if I've been drinking. Generally, as a rule, I try not to drink in the mornings. But as something inside me begins to sway, I have to wonder if I have somehow, unbeknownst to myself, strayed from that rule.

The eager woman—I feel that *eager* is very much the right word for her—returns her clipboard to her desk and comes out from behind it. She moves toward us quickly. Her step is a little skip, one that I suspect would like to be a big leaping skip if only the office size were more conducive to such happy movements. Her ponytail manages to bob with the two steps she does take. As I reach out to shake her outstretched hand, I notice that her two front teeth are very slightly bucked. She firmly shakes and quickly releases my hand and then reaches out to Renee.

"Amy, Renee, hi? It's great to meet you?" Erin says, or asks, it's hard to be sure. "I'm Erin Reiss? And I'm your executive producer? I'll be involved in literally every aspect of the show? I'll be with you whenever we're out on location and of course when we're here, on the set?"

"Excellent to meet you!" says Renee, and again I have the if-not-drunk-then-at-least-very-woozy feeling again.

"Great, thanks," I manage to offer.

"Great?" Erin exclaims, or inquires, I'm still not entirely sure. "And can I just say how excited we are? All of us here at DTV? We're so excited to have you on board? We think it's going to be a really great show? We're really going to be raising the bar in terms of pro-gramming for dogs?"

I nod.

"Fantastic!" Renee adds.

Erin smiles, with all her teeth, and I think of wood-chucks. As she bends down to pet Carlie and to speak in baby talk to her, I hope Carlie doesn't have the same impression, because I'm pretty sure a woodchuck could be considered part of the vermin family, and hunting vermin, well, that is, after all, Carlie's *raison d'etre*.

Erin's head pops back up a moment later. "And this is Barton?" she continues, gesturing again broadly, game-show-hostess-like to the other, darker side. "Barton is our director and also our writer." Barton steps forward, shakes our hands, and tells us very softly and very unconvincingly that he is pleased to meet us, and all but ignores Carlie. The word *director* means nothing to me. The only thing I hear is the word *writer.* I notice his slovenliness; it is a part of everything about him, the way he moves, the way he speaks, the way he seems never to have brushed his hair. I look at him intently and the word *writer* rings menacingly in my ears. I wonder if this is what happens to writers once they realize they're not going to write anything that matters. I wonder, is this how they end up? *Yes,* I think, *yes, maybe it is.*

I reach up to my ponytail. I separate it into two sections and pull the sections away from each other in an effort to smooth it. I reach down and run my hands over the front of my skirt, quick brushing motions. Once I've stood up a bit straighter and taken a deep, posture-enhancing breath, I reach out my hand to him. He takes it.

"It's very nice to meet you," I say. I'm starting to realize that what happens is that eventually all the little lies that don't seem to mean anything pile up and pile up, and at some point it simply becomes both impossible and pointless to even try to keep track of them.

"All right, then?" Erin says with a quick clap of her hands. "Let's go see the set first?"

"Oh," I say, "you already have the set?" I had not, when I had envisioned this, envisioned any part of it to be so far along as to include an actual set. Suddenly, I'm not sure I'm quite ready for the reality, or for anything else.

"Oh, absolutely?" Erin says, nodding her head enthusiastically, ponytail bobbing rhythmically in agreement. "We've been ready to go for a while? We just needed the dog?"

Carlie looks up quickly, fixes Erin in an intent gaze. I am less quick, less intent. I smile, nod, and I notice Barton widening his eyes at Erin.

"Oh," Erin adds on hastily, "and you?" She smiles broadly. "We needed you?"

I nod again, and Renee, Carlie, and I follow Erin and Barton out the door.

We walk down the hallway and through a black door to the set. There are three white leather chairs up on a carpeted platform. I think the white leather chairs might have been a mistake, what with Carlie being a dog and all, and also, Carlie is completely white. She photographs so much better against a black background. I do not say anything about that, mostly because I'm caught just slightly off guard by the fact that I just thought it. Somehow, I am able to reach into my innermost reserves where I find the strength to refrain from saying anything at all about the giant poster hanging from the ceiling as a backdrop to the set. It is of a giant purple Westie that

I imagine is supposed to be Carlie. I stare at the giant Carlie poster for a long moment, mesmerized. Its height, its width, the way it hangs so boldly from the ceiling. It's as if Carlie is the benevolent dictator of her very own country. Westiestan.

"All right, then?" Erin says again, and again she signals a continuation of our tour with a clap. All of us except for Barton, who somewhere along the way has disappeared, head out into the hall. As we exit, our group almost bumps into a man exiting quickly from the adjacent studio. He's quite tall, a little gangly, the type of person who takes up a lot of space. But there is something in his demeanor that suggests he's somehow sorry for that. He's hesitant, he looms. I think of Lurch. He looks down at us, hovering, lingering, and I feel as if we still would have bumped into him had he left the studio a moment earlier, or a moment later. Somehow, we would have collided no matter what. He's dressed strangely—or actually, he's dressed all in black like everyone else in New York. But there is something strange about him. His hair is long in the front and thick; the word *floppy* comes to mind and I think strangely and simultaneously of Hugh Grant's hair in *Four Weddings and a Funeral* and also of high school. I feel like I've seen him somewhere before.

"Hi, Nick?" Erin says, grinning up at him eagerly.

"Hey," he says, smiling quickly at her and then looking down at the floor. I wonder if he's part of our show. I can't say why because quite honestly I don't know why, but suddenly I want him to be a part of our show. He looks up again, and Erin doesn't introduce us, but he smiles. I think he smiles at me, and also, I think he might be wearing eyeliner. And then the moment is over, just like that, and Erin turns on her heel, and Renee turns, and I do too, and we all walk away.

"Is he on our show?" I ask Erin as we walk. I feel I have to ask. I tell myself that's only because I am so sure I've seen him before.

"Oh, no?" Erin says perkily, bouncing along as she walks. "That's Nick Williams? He's the host of that show, *I Really Liked the Eighties a Lot*? It tapes right over there, in the studio next to ours?" She points back to the adjacent black door out of which he had appeared.

"I see," I say. The seeing has surprised me. It has taken me quite completely off guard. I've thought for a while now that I'm not very good at seeing things anymore. I've begun to consider that I suffer from the emotional equivalent of night blindness. I think to myself that the information about a show called *I Really Liked the Eighties a Lot* could go a long way in terms of explaining the eyeliner, and maybe even the hair. Maybe I have been drinking.

"It's a really terrific show?" Erin asks/informs me. "He's very deadpan? Very sexy Frankenstein as VJ? He's brilliant? Have you ever seen his show?"

"No, I don't think so," I say, and a moment ago, I would have been certain that I had never in my life watched a cable television show about the eighties. Only now, I'd have to say I'm not so sure. "I don't think so," I say again, even though I'm pretty sure that Erin is no longer listening to me.

Sometime later, I am shown pages. They're not empty pages like all the pages that are mine. They're pages with crisp typing all over them. I'm asked to sign them, and I do. I remind myself that this is a good thing, that change is a good thing. It could be entirely possible that that is true. Yet somehow, I do not find myself at all compelled to exclaim, "My dog's going to be on TV!" Nor do I want to say anything at all along the lines of, "Me, me, I'm going to be on TV, too!" I do not feel the tickle of anticipation I had imagined I would feel. I do not have the expected literal and figurative sensation of doors opening up before me. In this moment, the only feeling I have is that later, at some point, I'm going to look back on all of this with regret.

6

(carlie)

Friends, How Many of Us Have Them?

Amy is still sleeping. I am waiting. I have found it works best if I wait until the buzzer goes off, and then once that happens, proceed with the greatest level of enthusiasm. That works well, I think. It is just, the waiting. I am not so keen on the waiting. What is there to do while we wait? I cannot think of anything. And yet. I pick up Seal Baby from where she rests on the far corner of the bed. I drop her on Amy's chest. Nothing. I wait.

On occasion, upon waking (regardless of the time), I have been known to do my quick *chomp-chomp*: the *chomp-chomp* of which we have already spoken, the one that translates quite easily, if only someone would listen, to "Pay attention to me!" Though in the past, the early-morning *chomp-chomp* has not ever been remarkably successful. Usually, it only results in my being told sleep-ily, in a froggy voice, to "be a good girl." I do not under-stand this. *Good?* What is this *good?* *Good* is not the right word at all. There are good dogs, and then there are great dogs. And I am one of the great ones.

The box with the numbers on it starts to play music! It is like the buzzer! But now is not the time to talk about the buzzer.

Amy does not open an eye, but rather she reaches out an arm, swatting at the number box, until the music stops. There is so much more I have to tell you, about how I am one of the great ones, about my youth, not only the youth I spent uptown, but the youth before that, in Cape May, New Jersey. But now is not the time.

Now the music has stopped playing. I have seen this happen before. This could go on, again and again, for quite some time. Music will play, there will be swatting, and the box will fall silent for some time, and then the cycle will repeat. It is really more than I can bear, espe-cially in the morning. I have always thought of the morn-ing as Carlie's time. It is my overall belief that a great amount of the time during the day could be classified as Carlie's time, and I think I'm right about that. But this, the morning, is really the most important time. With my morning walk and the Tompkins Square Park and all the other dogs, it is the essence, if you will, of Carlie's time, the very purest part of it. So, if you will excuse me.

"Get the coffee cup! Get the coffee cup! Get the coffee cup! Get the coffee cup! Get the coffee cup!" I say to Amy as I try, with some success, to lick as much of her face as possible. This may not come as the greatest of surprises to you, but what I want Amy to do is this: I want her to get up and put on the coffee. I want her to get her portable coffee cup, the one that she brings with us to the park. Once she has gotten the coffee cup, we are as good as there. I wind up. I swat at her face with my paw. Oftentimes, I forget that Amy does not generally appreciate the swatting paw.

"Carlie, no!" floats through the air, and then it is gone. I try to remember not to swat with the paw even though it makes me think that there is no justice. With all of the swatting of the number box, why is it so wrong if I engage in a little friendly swatting of the face?

Amy gets up and out of the bed. I bet it is to get the coffee cup! And it is.

And we are, all because of me, on our way.

"This is the best morning! This is the best morning! This is the best morning!" Every morning, I follow Amy quickly around our home, as the coffee brews and is put into the cup. Every morning, I repeat, "This is the best morning, this is the best morning, this is the best morning," again and again, even though she does not hear me. I repeat it because it is a truth. I repeat it because I am pretty sure that Amy does not think so.

At last we are out the door. At last we are on our way to the Tompkins Square Park. The actual walk *to the park* is not my favorite part. This is mostly due to the fact that Amy and I have some fundamental differences in our philosophies when it comes to walking. At times, Amy is not very open-minded; walking is one of those times. She is only able to see walking as walking, she is unable to see it for what it really is: a great and cherished opportunity for hunting and gathering. And sniffing. And, sometimes, I simply like to lick the pavement. But above all, the sniffing.

Soon (sooner in fact than I would have liked) we arrive at the Tompkins Square Park and the First Run dog run that is within it. This park, while it is not without its merits, has never felt the same to me as Central Park. Sometimes I miss Central Park. That is not at all to say that it is bad here, but sometimes I do miss it. I have the inclination to believe that Amy feels the same.

The First Run is a run, a large but fenced-in space, and Central Park, it was free. In Central Park, as soon as we reached the bend in the road by the sweeping brick stairs, we were on what was called the bridle path. At first, I had the greatest love for the bridle path because horse manure was everywhere. Later, the stable that was nearby closed down and the horse manure was not nearly as abundant and then my love was not as great. But still, I loved it there because there, I was free. Free! Free as we circled the bridle path, the joggers jogging around the reservoir, above us and to our left. We couldn't stay there long, because I believe that joggers are a great threat to our very happiness.

Next, we would head south, down toward a place called the Great Lawn and up a set of great stone stairs (I love all stairs) to a castle I heard called Belvedere and then through a place called the Ramble where it was all woods and wilds and I was supposed to be leashed in that place, but I was not, I was free. I was a wild thing there, I was.

I am happy now. Still, I would say I was happier then. It is said that the Westie, by nature, is quick to move on. It is said that the Westie never looks back. But that goes to show that what is said is not always right or always true, because (and maybe you'll think this has something to do with Amy or maybe you won't, but I think it does) I remember, and I look back.

However, it is not my intention to be so fond in my remembrances of Central Park that you will think that I do not care for the First Run, because I do care for it, I care for it quite a lot. Only I think I might care for it in the way that I imagine people sometimes care incorrectly for things: they think things could be better, they long for improvements upon the things they have, but yet, they don't wish to give them up. But even so, I care for it here, too. I meet my friends here. We meet here, and we run.

It is a more social place here than Central Park was, mostly because everyone is in one place. I have come to believe that this social aspect, the daily meeting of the friends, is off-putting to Amy. In Central Park, we walked alone. Here, I run, and Amy stands with all the other people, and the people like to talk to each other. I don't think Amy likes it very much at all.

Amy is not the most social of beings under even the very best of circumstances. This is something about her that I do not understand, something I would like to discuss with her if only she would listen to me. It is my belief that people should try to be social. Even if they are not quite the amiable creatures that Westies are, they should at least try. People have so much time to spend in the world. I have long felt it could only help them to have a little bit of company along the way.

I have come over to stand by Amy now. Just as I approach, her cell phone rings. It is because I am one of the great ones that I try my best not to object. It requires a very serious, very concerted effort not to bark at her, not to give her a quick *chomp-chomp* (as is my way) to remind her that *this, here, now,* is my time. It is not time for the cell phone. Previously I only knew it as the small rectangle annoyance that was held to the ear. Then, it became lost and I heard Amy say several times, into the larger version inside the home, "I have lost my cell phone, and I have to get another." I did not know exactly why she felt she had to get another, since the cell phone seems to be mostly a cause of annoyance, and of frustration. Its ring results frequently in a narrowing of Amy's eyes. You would think (would you not?) that Amy would have simply opted not to get another cell phone. But yet, here: another cell phone. Also, I know a full three seconds before it rings that it's going to ring.

While I have thus far refrained from barking, refrained even from *chomp-chomp*ing, I stare up at Amy diligently (a sign of protest) and I listen. It is Renee. I can hear everything Renee is saying through the phone. Renee is saying she thinks Amy should come up with some ideas of things to do in the city with your dog. I think a suggestion might be watching her run at the First Run without talking on the cell phone.

"Do you know?" Amy answers. "I don't really do that many things in the city with my dog."

She does not? I must wonder about this. I wonder what else there is. I wonder how much more awaits me.

"Right," Renee says, pausing, but only briefly as is her way. "Well, look at it as an opportunity. To do things in the city with your dog."

I have always had an instinctual dislike of Renee. She reminds me of a cat, or of a dog groomer. But right now, I feel I may need to reevaluate my feelings.

"I think it would be a really good idea," Renee continues, "I feel it would be an excellent show of good faith, if you did a little of the research, if you wrote down a list of good—no make that great—ideas for the show."

I am one of the great ones.

"I mean, sure, of course I want to help," Amy says, and hesitates. "But that writer?" she asks.

"The unkempt one?" Renee offers.

"Actually I think the word you might be looking for is *slovenly.*"

"His name is Barton," Renee says, a bit impatiently.

"Right, him. Barton. I'm just saying that he didn't seem like such a team player. He might not welcome the collaboration?" Amy offers.

"TV writers are all team players. It's the nature of the beast. It's a very group pursuit," Renee explains, and I sense that Amy is happy right now. It would be my guess that she is happy right now that she is not a TV writer, that she is not required on a daily basis to be a part of a group pursuit.

Amy's eyes begin to dart around, the way I have some-times seen them do when she is sitting at her desk in front of the white rectangle shape. I have come to think that she looks for words. I think she looks for something to say.

"Here's what I'm thinking," Renee explains, "maybe, since you haven't gotten very far on *Swim, Carlie, Swim!*—I mean, of course, correct me if you have?" Renee lingers, waiting. And then continues. "Maybe you might want to consider setting *Swim, Carlie, Swim!* in

New York City? And then you could do some research, *and* work on finishing up *Swim, Carlie, Swim!*" Renee suggests, and even I cannot help but linger for a moment on the almost sad optimism of the phrase "finishing up."

"Only, *Swim, Carlie, Swim!* takes place in Wyoming, on the most treacherous stretches of the Snake River," Amy says.

"What are they—Carlie and Robert Maguire—they're on a white-water raft?" Renee asks.

"Kayak. I think they're on a kayak now," Amy tells her flatly.

"I thought they were rafting?"

"I switched it."

"That's great then, even better! What about if Carlie and Robert Maguire rent a kayak over by Chelsea Piers? I mean talk about super geographically convenient, right? Beyond. And maybe that could be something you and Carlie do together *in the city*? Two birds, one stone."

Birds?! Where? I look up to the sky, but I see nothing. I watch as Amy looks down, not even at me, but directly at the ground. After a moment she looks away from the ground, and up, and straight ahead. I can see her breathing slow breaths. The way she looks off into the distance like that makes me think of how she does not hear me, how maybe she does not listen. The way she's looking right now, just staring away at nothing, I wonder if sometimes, also, she doesn't see.

"It's not really about that," Amy says after a short while. "I'm not saying I won't do research for *Things to Do in the City with Your Dog* if that's what you think is best, but I can't combine the two. *Swim, Carlie, Swim!* has to take place outside New York, far outside New York, like all the others. That's a non-negotiable."

"Yes, well," Renee says.

"I don't think Robert Maguire has ever even set foot in New York," Amy continues, still looking/not looking at whatever is unseeable on the horizon. "Scotland, Paris, the Congo. All the *Run, Carlie, Run!* books take place outside New York. In a way," she adds, tilting her head in the way I sometimes do when I am sorting things out, "all the books are about leaving New York."

"Interesting," Renee says, and through the cell phone, I can hear the *tick-tick-tick* of a pen banging rhythmically against a table. "That might be something you might want to explore."

"It might be," Amy agrees. "Renee?" she says, after a moment.

"Yes?"

"I don't know, and I know it's a little late to bring this up, but ever since going to the studio? I don't know if I can exactly put my finger on it, but there's something about this show that's starting to leave a bad taste in my mouth."

I am inclined to reflect for a moment on the taste in

my own mouth: Newman's Own Organics Turkey and Brown Rice Dinner for Dogs. With a touch of pavement!

Renee tells Amy she should not worry and that she should think about that list and then, at last, the cell phone call is over.

As soon as the cell phone is safely put away, I turn. And I run!

7

(amy)

I Don't Know If It's You or If It's Me

As we enter the studio, the stage is dark. The cameras and confounding equipment have been left listless in front of the stage, bent over like electronic fossils, their wires crisscrossing each other like snakes. Erin is wearing a bright purple shift dress. The shade matches almost perfectly with the giant purple Carlie propaganda poster. I am in my dressiest and most professional pantsuit. Though to be technically correct, due to the fact that I work inside the home, it is my only pantsuit. I spent thirty-five minutes this morning straightening my hair. Carlie is resplendent in her turquoise bandana. I can't even begin to think of all the reasons why.

"Oh, Amy?" Erin says, turning toward me. "I've been meaning to ask you. Dodge? I know it's kind of a common name and all, but you wouldn't happen to be related to the Dodge Antiques family, would you?"

I stop in my tracks, unhappy to be reminded that as big as New York is, it can sometimes be the smallest place in the world. I stare blankly for a moment without saying a word, a deer that somehow wandered into the city only to get trapped there in the headlights.

"I only ask because my parents are collectors and have been clients of Dodge's for *years*?"

I consider lying. The only reason I don't is because of the apparent smallness of the world, or at least of New York. "I was related," I say. *Was*, the past tense of *be*. There it is, the past tense, I am in fact quite good at using it. "Um," I continue, "I was married to Jonathan Dodge. I'm not anymore."

"I know Jonathan!?" she exclaims, as if it's just the happiest coincidence in the world, as if I have not just now designated him as my ex-husband, but rather as some mutual chummy old pal. She says his name, *Jonathan*, as if this person we have in common is a cause for rejoicing, rather than the man who kept all the furniture because as it turned out, none of it was ever mine. I don't say anything. I offer up only a wan smile to her toothy, exuberant one. And in the loaded, filled-up (I really don't want to say *pregnant*) pause that follows, I wonder how just one question can change so many things.

"All right, then?" Erin says at last. She smiles fake-warmly at the assembled group of us, and claps, "Let's meet!" I can't help thinking that the clapping, though perhaps meant to be unifying, wasn't altogether necessary, seeing as in the time it took for Erin's brief journey down memory lane, Barton and I have climbed into the director's chairs that have been set up in a circle in front of the darkened stage.

Barton, dressed very much like a writer on a deadline who will be neither showering nor leaving the house any time in the foreseeable future, glances in the direction of Carlie with his heavy-lidded eyes. He puts me in mind of a mud-puddle-seeking hippopotamus. He pantomimes leaning down and picking up an imaginary Carlie-sized dog and depositing her into the empty director's chair between us. I notice as he does it that the chair between us actually says "Carlie" across the back. I hesitate for a moment and then I hop off my chair and situate Carlie in hers. As I return to my seat, I feel I can't do this without offering up just a bit of damage control.

"Um," I say to Barton, and I can feel all the eyes in the room on me. "I'm not altogether sure Carlie will stay in her own director's chair." It's not actually that I worry that she'll jump off it or worse, fall off it and hurtle the three, four feet to the floor. While Carlie does have a touch of the klutz (it's true, she really does), I've only seen it come out on the upswing. When she's trying to jump onto a bed, occasionally she'll misjudge and fall back down. She's lost her footing once or twice on the way up a stair, but once she's up on something, a ledge of any sort, a precipice, anything with any degree of height (a precarious perch atop La Tour Eiffel comes to mind), she's quite steady.

I worry more that she simply won't care for being put in said director's chair, and her displeasure will result in the emitting of one of Carlie's patented, well-practiced Westie screams. It's true. If Carlie doesn't like the way things are going, if someone startles her, if a dog in the park is gaining on her, or heaven forbid, actually outrunning her, if a person is trying to enjoy a stack of saltine crackers without giving her at least several, she will emit a startling and ear-piercing scream. It's not a bark, it's not a growl, it is without question a scream. The Westie, it is said, will not be ignored.

"Okay, first order of business?" Erin says with a sidelong glance at Barton. "We're thinking of changing the spelling of *Amy*?"

What's that? I look up at Erin. "I'm sorry?"

"That's okay?" she says soothingly. She reaches her hand out as if to touch my arm, or maybe just the armrest of my chair. But our chairs are too far apart so her hand just hangs there strangely in the air between us.

"No," I say. "I meant, I'm sorry but could you repeat that?"

Erin only smiles at me sweetly, blinking more than is probably necessary. I look over at Barton. His eyes dart quickly from me over to Erin, who is now staring down at her clipboard. I watch as her eyes move from left to right, and I want to know what's on that clipboard. She writes something down. Her pen is topped with a fluffy plume, like a troll doll's hair. As she flips a page, the crinkling sound of the rustling paper carries in the cavernous space.

I look away, over at Carlie, who is sitting quite still in her director's chair, watching the action intently. I close my eyes for a moment. In my mind I see a blackboard; it's the type of blackboard that's actually dark green instead of black. Written across it in chalk—big white block letters—are the words MY LIFE.

"Right?" Erin says, not looking up from her clipboard. "What we're thinking of is changing the spelling of *Amy*?

"A-m-i-e?" Barton offers helpfully. "With an -ie?" he concludes.

"We think it would look much better to have a lot of -ie going on? *Carlie,* of course, and *Amie*?" she explains in a manner of utmost seriousness. She then nods enthusiastically and sways ever so slightly in her chair. "Really brilliant, right?" I look at her blankly. I myself blink a few more times than may be considered absolutely necessary. "Barton!?" she says next, whipping around quickly in her chair. "You know!? We could even use that song, 'Amie,' for the introduction?!" She starts scribbling furiously on her clipboard. The troll hair shakes rhythmically.

Erin turns back to me and speaks slowly, as if to a youngster. "Amy, that's the part of the show that's, you know, the same every week? The part of the show where a theme song would be played?"

"Right," I say, and then, and I really can't emphasize enough how much I hate it when this happens, Erin bursts into song.

"Amie, what you wanna do?"

My next thought is that I hate her.

"What are your thoughts?" Barton asks me, suddenly reemerging from his own slothlike perpetual waking sleep.

"My thoughts?" I ask back.

"Yes, just right off the top of your head, you know, like brainstorming?" Erin replies. With the dancing cadence of her tone, the amount of happy emphasis placed on the word *brainstorming*, you'd think she were saying *ice cream. Christmas. Puppies.* And she's staring at me with eager overenthusiasm again.

"Thank you, Barton," I say, turning to face him completely. "My *thought*," I begin, placing my own emphasis on the singular nature of the word *thought*, "is that my name is spelled with a Y, and that's how it's spelled on the books. All the *Run, Carlie, Run!* books."

At the mention of the books, both Erin and Barton break out into grins. I wasn't aware of feeling that they didn't like me until now, when a mention of the books seems to make them like me again.

"We love the *Run, Carlie, Run!* books?" Erin says.

"We do," Barton says. "We loved the tone."

"We love the happy sense of adventure? We love Carlie and we love Robert Maguire?" Erin gushes.

"Thanks," I say.

"But we think *Amie* with an -ie is the all-around better way to go with this?" Erin adds.

I don't say anything. I think of when Jonathan and I named Carlie. Jonathan had liked the spelling *Carleigh*. I didn't and amended it to *Carlie*, explaining to Jonathan that when I thought of Carlie, I thought of it spelled a particular way. He told me he wasn't sure we'd ever see eye to eye on anything. It dawned on me then that I might not ever name a baby, that I might only ever name Carlie, and so I insisted on *Carlie*, and for that moment it hadn't been about Carlie at all.

"We think *Amie* with an -ie is really all-around better?" Erin repeats again, grinning at me in a way I am now tempted to call maniacally.

"Right," I say, and as soon as I do, I notice Barton glancing over awkwardly at Erin.

"Right, yes?" Erin says oddly, with an almost pained look. Carlie is following everyone's glances, her eyes traveling intently from person to person to person, from look to look to look.

"Amy?" Erin continues, and I wonder how she's spelling it in her mind, and I think most likely it's with an -ie. I can't shake the feeling that I've been passed around for comment, and changed, all of it without any need for input from me. "Amy, the reason we're here?" she asks me. Everything is a question. She poses all these questions as if she somehow thinks I am the one who has the answers rather than the one who feels she's already been waiting quite awhile for them. I don't say anything. I have no idea what to say. I feel my hand instinctively go up to my hair. As I catch myself and force my hand back down to my lap, I am reminded of the way that Carlie will lift her left foot up, holding it above the ground pointer-style at times. I've never been sure if she does this because she's confused or scared, or on the hunt.

"We need to talk to you about something?" Erin continues slowly, still looking far too eagerly at me, focused on me completely. I keep my hands in my lap, away from my hair, and wish that Erin would look down at her clipboard, gaze upon her fluffy pen, if only for a moment; I feel it would lessen the intensity and I feel it would be so much better that way.

"Right, okay," I say.

"This isn't something we've decided lightly, and we don't want you to take it personally?" is her lead-in. In the history of lead-ins, I'm pretty sure that "We don't want you to take it personally" hasn't ever preceded anything good. I nod. I am compelled somehow not to look away, compelled to meet her clear-eyed gaze.

"We've decided to recast the character of Amie?" she says next, making quotes in the air with her fingers when she says the word *character*.

There is a moment, a beat, before my brain makes the leap from *Amy* to *Amie* to "the character of Amie," before it can wrap itself around the concept. And then it does. In the next eager instant, Erin has leaned all the way forward in her chair.

"We've hired a really lovely young actress named Bonnie Beller?" *Hired* is the word that's bold and loud in my mind. *Hired*, I think, past tense, done. I close my eyes for a second. I'm done. I open my eyes. "She's really brilliant?" Erin continues. "She used to be the host of the self-help show *Embrace the Happy*? Did you ever get a chance to see it? It was really wonderful?"

"No," I say, "I've never seen *Embrace the Happy*." Erin nods slowly, sympathetically, understandingly.

"We need to start filming," she says in a soothing voice that I fail to find soothing at all, "if we have any hope of staying on schedule? And like I said, she's really lovely? People loved her on *Embrace the Happy*?"

"I'm sorry," I say, misspeaking again, though this time maybe I am a little bit sorry. "I mean, is this something you can do? I think I need to talk to Renee." I keep talking, to no one in particular. "Why isn't Renee here? Does Renee know about this?"

Erin simply stares back at me, clear-eyed, smiling much more serenely now, as though if enough time passes I'll naturally come to see that this is for the best, that a fictional version of me is so much better than the real one. It occurs to me that maybe this is not any different at all from my preferring Robert Maguire to any of the men I've ever met in New York, my ex-husband included. I meet Erin's stare.

"I don't know if this is what I signed up for," I say.

"Actually?" Erin says, her toothy smile disappearing, evaporating completely to a thin line, one that says it shouldn't be crossed. "It's exactly what you signed up for?" She uses air quotes again around the words *signed up*, and continues, "Page four of your contract, paragraph two?" She enunciates each syllable. My mind flashes back to Renee flipping pages around, saying, "It's fine, it's pretty standard for television."

I look down at my lap, my pantsuit. They were disappointed in me, they didn't want me. They were disappointed in even the most spruced-up version of me. But maybe everyone is always disappointed in everyone. Maybe we all just want fiction because the real thing can have such a way of falling so terribly short. Maybe this is the universe's way of telling me it's okay that Robert Maguire is as firmly lodged in my psyche as he is? But really, does the universe have that kind of time?

"*Embrace the Happy* has been off the air for about a year and a half now, so it's a great time for Bonnie to be returning to the screen. She'll seem fresh and new but still familiar?" Erin explains, and I wonder, can this be it? Is this conversation actually moving on? Is there nothing I can do to stop it? Again, I think of that dark-green blackboard with the words MY LIFE written across it in block letters. Only, what I missed the first time was that my name, spelled correctly, was written out underneath it. AMY. What I missed the first time is that someone— or something—I can't see is slowly and methodically erasing my name.

"It's only been off the air a year and a half?" Barton asks. "I thought it was longer?"

Erin shoots him a look. He catches it and looks away. "Yes," Erin agrees, "it seems like longer, doesn't it? But no, Bonnie had her thing a year and a half ago?"

"What thing?" I ask.

"She kind of had a nervous breakdown," Barton tells me.

"A nervous breakdown?"

"Barton?" Erin interrupts. "I think that's such a negative term, don't you? And I think it sounds as if it's from the nineteen fifties and it really sends the wrong message?" She turns to me. "She was struggling with depression?" I think what I imagine anyone would think: but she was the host of *Embrace the Happy*? "But she's fine now, doing great. Turns out that for the most part it was nothing more than a little undiagnosed chronic fatigue syndrome?"

"Uh-huh," I say. I wonder if right now it might be the only thing in the world to say.

"Really," Erin adds, "she's really very sweet? Very lovely? I'm sure you'll really like her a lot?" I doubt that. "Which will be great," Erin adds, "because Bonnie has expressed an interest in spending some time with you so that she can stay as true to your character as possible?" I think that I really need to get Renee on the phone as soon as humanly possible. And I think also that I'd like to leave now.

"Amy?" Erin continues, and could there possibly be more? I wonder if maybe there is, if maybe she'll keep talking forever. "I understand this may be upsetting to you? But think about it this way? You would have just been speaking lines that we wrote for you? And wearing clothes that we picked out for you? So how different really is it if it's not *technically* you?"

"Erin," I say. "I think it's pretty different."

"Well? I don't think it's so different? And I think the change will make for some really great television?"

"I'm going to leave now," I say. It comes out sounding a bit more dramatic than I intended.

As I excuse myself, as I pick Carlie up off the chair and place her on the floor, I think that I'd like to be anywhere else. Maybe London. I'd like to walk through the streets in the rain. I'd like to take Carlie to see Parliament, to see Big Ben, and Buckingham Palace. I'd like to be perfectly still, and safe, and not in any sort of danger at all. I'd like for there not to be any reason at all for anyone to say, "Run, Carlie, run!"

As Carlie and I walk away from the circle the conversation does not linger on my being recast, but returns again to my name.

"Also, Barton?" Erin says, and I turn back around to see her extending her arms languidly over her head in a cat stretch. I think that a cat stretch is really unapropos, given the reason we're all here. "Maybe instead of *Amie*, what about *Abilene*? I've always loved the name *Abilene*, haven't you?"

"Oh, I have," Barton says, and I think, *really*? "That's something to think about."

I am compelled once again to speak. I walk, with Carlie, the few steps back to the circle of director's chairs I was only moments away from escaping. Erin and Barton look up at me curiously. Their expressions are both a perfect, possibly practiced mix of expectancy and dismissal.

"Only," I begin, "wouldn't you think of someone named Abilene as being from Texas? Wouldn't you think it's a really Texan name, seeing as it's a Texan city and all?" They stare at me blankly, as if I have arrived in this conversation uninvited and from nowhere. "And I'm not Texan," I conclude.

"Amy," Erin says softly, and I notice that her voice isn't rising. I don't hear any question mark on the end. "I think it's really important to remember that you're no longer you."

8

I'm Mr. Blue (I'm Here to Stay with You)

At the moment, all I'm able to say about Renee is that right now is not the time that will ever be looked at as the highlight of our up-until-now-mostly-very-pleasant working relationship. Beyond that, I suspect that any other words spoken on the subject could very well be looked back on with regret. And also, I'm too preoccupied.

Bonnie Beller, recently of seventeen episodes of *Embrace the Happy*, and even more recently of an episode with mental health (that's what we're calling it now, so said Erin) is on the soundstage, with the giant purple Carlie poster behind her, running lines. I have yet to meet her, and I can't say that our meeting is an event to which I'm greatly looking forward. Although I am aware that none of this is technically her fault, and that this Bonnie may in fact have some real problems of her own, that maybe she might even be in need of some sympathy, I don't want to meet her. I'd like to avoid her forever if possible, usurper that she is.

In the last forty-eight hours, Bonnie Beller has become to me the human equivalent of any book that has ever knocked *Run, Carlie, Run!* down a notch on a bestseller list; she is any fictional character that has been featured in this review or that review, praised as *original, authentic, fresh,* when Carlie and Robert Maguire have been overlooked.

And while I'm obviously fine with the fact that my introduction to Bonnie has not been high on the list of anyone's priorities, for the record, I do take issue with the fact that no one has come to introduce Carlie to Bonnie. Instead of partaking in any introductions on the soundstage, Carlie and I are here, out in the hallway with Love. Love is the stylist for the show. Love is a remarkably pale woman whose midriff is exposed between low-slung jeans and a too-short T-shirt. Her exposed hip bones jut out at me aggressively. She has both a walkie-talkie and a pair of silver scissors attached to her by way of her belt loops, and her left wrist is covered for a span of at least three inches, maybe more, by a black leather band. Love has most recently come over, introduced herself to me, and explained with a straight face that Carlie is needed in Makeup. Things I've learned so far in my new life as a star of cable television: (1) I am not going to be a star of cable television; Bonnie Beller is. (2) Renee is never to be forgiven. (3) Here, makeup is a place.

Carlie looks hard at Love and then at me. I am sure the way she looks at me is meant to imply that should I agree to this, I, too, will find myself among those never to be forgiven. I'm not sure she'd understand me were I to say to her that the fact that I have already agreed to some other things makes it so that I don't have much of a choice when it comes to agreeing to this. Love, whose hair is the jet-black color beloved by Goth teenagers and vampire brides, eyes Carlie's leash in my hand.

"Can I come?" I ask, realizing the moment the words have left my mouth that I'm putting the power in the wrong place. I want the power to be in the right place, or rather in *my* place. "I'd like to stay with her," I say and as I say it, I know it's one of the only truths of my life. The one thing I know, the one thing I am sure will never change is the fact that I would always like to stay with Carlie. I know this with the same certainty that I know this woman, Love, whom I already distrust if only because of her inherently hostile choice of hair color, is going to tell me that's not a good idea.

"I don't think that's a good idea," Love tells me. Maybe I was never meant to be a writer at all. Maybe what I really am is a psychic.

"I know," I say, and her eyes focus a bit harder on me, and then again on Carlie's leash. I hold it tighter. "But I'd really rather come with her."

Love pops a piece of heretofore-concealed hot-pink bubble gum at me and informs me, "I've done a lot of work with animals before." In the right context, delivered with the right tone, such a statement could be reassuring, or even kind. In this instance it's not. I stare back at Love in a way that I hope conveys an unyielding sense of purpose.

"Uh-huh," I answer in a tone I hope is of the utmost inflexibility.

"Really, you have to trust me," she continues, and a sweetness creeps into her voice. "It's so much better for the animals to be bathed one-on-one," she explains. The way she says *animals* instead of *dogs* strikes me as impersonal. I think of Love in a shower stall hosing down an ostrich. "Do you want to talk to Erin about it?" she asks me next. I really don't want to talk to Erin about it, though I tell myself that's not the reason I will give in.

I try to work with the small voice in my head, the one that at times I am sure is wise, and most other times I just try to ignore. It is telling me to pull it together, to recall the many times that Carlie has been dropped off at the groomer's for a shampoo and a haircut, and returned just fine, how it's never a big deal, how Carlie doesn't even seem to mind the groomer's. I try to agree with the voice in my head. There could be logic there.

I smile down at Carlie. I try to convey to her, as much as to myself, that really, it's fine. I hand over Carlie's leash and she looks up at me—shocked—as she is led away. I take a few steps over to the wall. I turn around and lean back against it.

I open up my bag and look down into it. There, next to my folded newspaper, is my well-worn copy of *The Great Gatsby*. I carry it around with me to remind myself that in the beginning, when everything ended and had to be started all over again, my goal had been to write a novel, and a Great American Novel at that. I think I carry it around for other reasons, too.

When I left Jonathan on the Upper East Side, I took a lot of books with me. At the very last minute, I said I'd like to take some of the books. And in our case it really was the very last minute. Jonathan had packed books up into a box for me and also, separately, he had handed me a navy-blue paperback and I'd said, "Oh, *The Great Gatsby*, thanks." He'd nodded and smiled in a way I felt sure was sadly. It had confused me then because I'd come to believe there was a villain in all of this and that Jonathan was the villain, except in that moment he didn't seem like one at all.

I lean back against the wall and I close my eyes for a moment. I hear a door opening, a slight and tinny and nearby screech of an announcement. I open my eyes, and there, right in front of me, is the host from the eighties show, the *I Really Liked the Eighties a Lot* guy. I stare for a moment at his blue eyes, the almost bluish tint to his black hair, the blue that seems to be lurking just underneath his skin. Everything about him seems blue.

Nick Williams. His name runs across my mind. I think it's a nice enough name, pleasant-sounding, and I wonder if they changed his name, too.

"Amy, right?" he asks nodding, and then adds, "hey."

I focus more on the blue metallic of his eyeliner than I focus on the blue metallic of his eyes and reply, "Hey," myself. I sometimes think there's something friendlier about just saying *hey* and not adding on someone's name. Though such a random rule might apply only if you actually already know a person, and then really all I've accomplished here is coming off as standoffish. I do that. He smiles at me a bit awkwardly. I wonder if it's maybe like he'd rather be somewhere else. I have that same feeling again, the feeling that I've seen him somewhere before.

"It is Amy, right?" I look into his eyes, and it occurs to me that he looks sad; not sad right now, but more historically sad. "Yes," I say, "it's Amy."

"Amyyyyyyyy!" I hear, loud and bubbly and boisterous, coming at me from behind, filling up the hall completely. I turn around and see a tall, thin, beautiful blond woman walking toward me, her right arm outstretched, leading the way. "Bonnie Beller!" she announces. "I am just sooo happy to meet you!" She grabs my hand forcibly, shakes it vigorously.

I take in the luminosity of her skin and the golden blond of her hair. I've always thought of myself as a blonde. I've liked being a blonde, too. But now, as I look at this woman's hair, bright blond with many artfully placed even lighter blond streaks, I wonder if all these years I've been wrong and my hair is actually a shade much closer to gray. Her hair has been carefully, meticulously styled so that each wave looks as if it had been lovingly wrapped around someone's finger and carefully, gracefully twirled. I imagine it was.

I look closer. She does look a little like me. Only she's a thoroughly amped-up version of me. I'm five-six. She's five-eight and her limbs are thin and very long, much thinner, much longer than mine. Her arms bring to mind the word *willowy*. My skin is fair; hers is alabaster. My eyes are gray; hers are bright blue. I could go on. I could compare bra sizes. I could talk about youth, and crow's-feet. But I won't.

"Bonnie, hi. It's nice to meet you," I say, expert liar that I have become.

And then, though everything that is logical and self-preserving in the world tells me I should not, I turn and introduce her to Nick.

"Bonnie, this is Nick. Nick, Bonnie," I speak quickly. I think if I say their names fast enough, maybe he won't notice how very long her legs are, won't notice how she puts one in mind of complicated yoga poses simply by standing there, how she seems so young. I wonder what happened to her nervous breakdown, her depression, her mental-health episode? It seems impossible to me that anyone so very beautiful and so very bubbly could have any of those things.

"Oh, hey, yeah," Bonnie says, bobbing her head, a full, shoulder-including bob. She points a finger out to Nick, her thumb cocked up, in the shape of a handgun. *"I Really Liked the Eighties a Lot,* right?"

"Yeah," Nick says. I am pleased to see that he does not appear instantly mesmerized; neither lost nor swimming longingly in the lakelike blue of her eyes. He looks up and extends a hand to her. "Nick Williams, nice to meet you."

"Terrific show, man," she says, coolly. She is the type of person who can actually get away with saying *man*. I could add that to my Amy/Bonnie comparative list if I weren't already so sure that nothing good could come out of such a list.

"Thanks," Nick says, and I feel relieved as he excuses himself and heads down the hall, away from us. I turn again to Bonnie, who is still smiling happily at me, and who seems like a very nice person. I feel like a not-very-nice person at all, and the feeling is only magnified, highlighted by the way she has lit up the room, or rather, the hallway.

"So, wow, right," she says, nodding, bobbing. "I'm so excited to be working with you, and I'm super excited to get to know you."

"Mmm, hmm," I say, noncommittally, unenthusiastically, and as she smiles back at me, unperturbed, I once again feel not very nice at all. I should be nicer than this. Actually, I *am* nicer than this; I'm from Colorado, after all. I know that being from Colorado doesn't guarantee niceness: I know that there are probably plenty of not-very-nice people who hail from my state, but in this moment, reminding myself that I am, after all, a Coloradoan, makes me somehow feel better. I think of when I first moved to New York, how everyone seemed so unfriendly and so well dressed, how I wanted to be anything but a Boulderite. I wanted to be the way I had imagined my parents must have been before they left. I wanted to be from here, a lifelong New Yorker. Only right now I don't want to be a New Yorker, and really, not like this. "Right," I add, forcing myself to smile. "I'm looking forward to getting to know you, too."

"Really?" she says. "Oh, really, really good!" She grabs my hand again, shakes it again, smiles widely and brightly and all-consumingly down at me again. "Because, you know, I was a little worried, that there'd, you know, maybe be bad blood, and I'm so glad there's not."

I smile again, and this smile, it might be a bit more forced than the last one. I wonder when Carlie will be back.

"So, great, right?" Bonnie continues. "Now, this weekend, Saturday, unfortunately I'm booked. Alas, right? Big sigh! But how about Sunday? Could I come over then? I was thinking maybe like every Sunday, if that's cool?"

"Sunday?" I repeat.

"Yay! Sunday! Great! Okay, you know, I don't want to get in your way or anything. I mean like maybe we could have brunch or lunch or even dinner sometimes. Or see a movie! I love to see movies. Just about any movie. As long as it has a happy ending, you know? Nothing with violence or explosions or death, because I think there's enough of that already in the real world." She nods at me seriously. I nod back. I'm not sure what else to do. She continues. "But right. I don't want to get in your way. I mean, like I said, I would just love to hang out but if you'd like to do your own thing, I want you to do your own thing. I don't know what your thing is. But I'm looking forward to getting to know. But say it's like yoga? Awesome, I'll come with! Or if it's the gym, I'll come, too, though I do have to say that I think yoga is such a better way to exercise than anything else that's out there. It's such a more fostering and nurturing process and it's so much kinder and gentler and more in touch with the human spirit. And I think it's so important to be in touch with the human spirit. I really feel that too many people aren't in touch with their spirits and if only they were, the world would have a lot less problems." She pauses, takes a deep breath, closes her eyes for a moment. She opens them. "Or maybe on Sundays, do you write? You're a writer, right? That is so cool. You must write all the time. I could just come over and hang while you write. If that's cool?"

I wait until I am sure she's done speaking before I close my eyes myself for a moment. I think, *This can't be my life*. And then Bonnie reaches out and grabs my hand again. She doesn't shake it. She just holds it in between her two hands. She is so earnest, so completely free of social convention. And so interested in me. Slowly, I nod my head and say, "Okay."

"Oh, great!" she says. "Really great. And I was thinking, you know, maybe once or twice, I could sleep over?"

Before I can address that, before my reclusive and solitary brain can wrap itself around any of this, Carlie returns. She is fluffed and coiffed from a bath. Also, she's looking a bit fierce because they've trimmed her around her eyes, and she always winds up looking a bit fierce when they do that, and I think that maybe someone should have asked me before they went ahead and trimmed around her eyes.

"Hi, Carlie!" Bonnie says in a very high voice, bending down quickly to be at eye level. And Carlie, ever the sucker for the very high voice, puts her ears back and wags her tail quickly. To my slight dismay, she twirls around a bit with the side of her face on the floor and her tail in the air, while grunting. It is a dance move of Carlie's that, because it reminds me of Arte Johnson's portrayal of Renfield to George Hamilton's Dracula in *Love at First Bite,* I have come to think of as "Renfield." "Renfield" means Carlie really likes someone. "Renfield" means she's quite overcome with adoration. *Et tu, Carlie?*

"All right then, beauty girl," Bonnie says to Carlie, "you want to go inside and tape a show?" Carlie continues with the Renfield, and I think, *Really, Carlie, it's enough with the Renfield.* Love—she's here too, she brought Carlie back—hands off Carlie's leash to Bonnie. She hands the leash to Bonnie, not to me, and I know it's all a TV show, and I know it's not real, but for a second I feel like I might die.

"Amy," Bonnie says, standing up to her full height again. "You should come watch."

"Thanks," I say, as nicely as I can, taking care to remind myself that none of this is Bonnie's fault, that I am originally from Colorado, and that sometimes Carlie will bust out into Renfield even when no one's around. Only that last part isn't true. "But I think I'll wait out here. I don't want Carlie to get distracted."

"Are you sure?"

"Sure, I'm sure," I say, and I lean down and pick up my bag. I hold it up to her. "I brought a book with me, I've got some reading to do." I don't actually take the book out of the bag. I don't actually ever take the book out of the bag.

"Okay, then," she says. I walk them as far as the door to the studio, and then I occupy myself with pretending to dig in my bag, so I don't have to watch Carlie walking away with the new Amy. Or rather, Amie. Or maybe now it's Abilene. I should check.

Eventually I take the newspaper out of my bag, though I don't get very much reading done. But somehow it does happen; somehow, very slowly, the day comes to an end. And I do wonder once or twice over the course of the long, hanging-out-alone-in-the-hallway day, if I will see Nick again. So when I do see him standing outside as Carlie and I exit the studio, right there in my line of vision, with the Fifty-ninth Street Bridge and Manhattan stretching out behind him, I am not only pleasantly surprised but also of the mind that it might be ever-so-slightly cosmic.

"Hi again," I say as Carlie and I approach.

"Hi, Amy," he says, and then, bending down, he reaches out to pet Carlie. "And you must be Carlie, I don't think we've properly met." Carlie barks at him. I wonder if she's protecting me, if there's something she inherently knows that I don't know, or if she's just barking because he is a little Lurch-like. And then, as Nick stands up to his full height again, I tell myself I shouldn't call him Lurch-like, even if only in the recesses of my mind. Lurch was probably close to seven feet tall, and this man is what, six feet, maybe six-one tops, it's just that New York is a short city. That's all. That, and there is something about him that's looming. And he does have a way of just appearing.

"Heading to the subway?" he asks, and since Carlie and I are car-service-less this time, I tell him that indeed we are. I notice that his T-shirt has writing on it but the straps of his backpack are covering some of the words so I can't read it. I'd like to know what it says. The not knowing makes me feel too much like maybe there's a joke I'm not getting.

At the entrance to the F train I stoop down to attempt the wrangling of Carlie into her Sherpa bag. She resists mightily. I wonder if with all the things piling up, the many bones I have to pick with Renee, if I can add to that list the fact that Carlie would so much prefer to travel by car service. I wonder if it would de-legitimize my other complaints.

As Nick and I descend into the station and stand waiting on the subway platform, I wonder where he lives. I consider whether it would be stalkerish to ask. I'm guessing no, but I don't ask anyway.

Once the train arrives, we take a seat next to each other, the two seats closest to the front of the car. I sit with the Sherpa bag in my lap and unzip a portion of zipper. Carlie pops her head out and stares at me wild-eyed, tongue flailing. I smile at her, I pat her head. "Shh, honey," I say, even though she's not making any noise.

There isn't any conversation, but it isn't an awkward silence. I notice Nick is looking expectantly around the car. It could be that he's looking to see if there's anyone on the train who is pregnant, or elderly, or infirm, who might need him to offer up his seat. Or it could be he's looking around to see if someone has a gun, a bomb, some sort of transit threat. I don't yet know. I don't yet know what kind of person he is. I try to look at him out of the corner of my eye. I don't want him to notice.

He looks down at the floor of the subway car. For someone whose job it is to be on TV, to host a show, he's not a very outward person. I wouldn't say withdrawn, because there is a spark in his eyes that makes me think *withdrawn* would be the wrong word. But yet there's something very inward about him. And though there is clearly something about him that I do find charming, I'm not sure it's a universal thing, I'm not sure everyone would. I look closer. He's not a charmer. He's not the leading man or the type likely to be assigned the role of hero. And while that might seem like a lot to be able to tell by looking at someone, I can tell. I can tell because in so many ways, I'm exactly the same way.

Later, after we ascend the stairs into Union Square and Carlie is at last freed from the bondage of her bag, Nick indicates with a cocked thumb that he's headed uptown, or at least farther uptown than Fourteenth Street.

"So, I'm that way," he says.

"We're that way," I say, waving vaguely, indicating points south. Nick doesn't turn to go, he's just standing there. And then I realize, so am I.

"Nick?" I say.

"Yes?"

"What does your shirt say?"

"Oh," he says. He slides one shoulder out of his backpack, and holds the front of his shirt out away from his body so that I can read it. He seems pleased to have been asked.

"'When you're lonely, I'll be lonely, too,'" I read out loud. "Oh," I say, "that's really nice." I think it is.

"It's Yaz," he says.

"Yaz?"

"Short-lived but highly successful synthpop duo from Essex?" he asks, in a surely-you-know-what-I'm-talking-about way.

"Right," I say, nodding in a way that I hope conveys vast musical knowledge. I don't think I have ever before in my life wanted to convey vast musical knowledge. "Right. Sure, I know Yaz. Which song is that from?"

"Mr. Blue."

"Oh," I say. I don't know what to say, and a song I haven't heard in two decades filters slowly back into my consciousness. I wonder if that's how every moment is for Nick.

He looks at me for a second and hesitates like he's trying to figure out what to say or how to say it. I think he's not the type of man to always know just what to say, to handily, snappily deliver a punch line. He is perhaps not the quickest on his feet. I'm not so sure his timing would be swift enough to know when to call out, "Run, Carlie, run!" before anything went too terribly wrong. I have no idea why I just thought that, but as I do, I realize that this man, standing here, tall and dark and blue in front of me, is nothing at all like Robert Maguire.

"Amy?" he says.

"Uh-huh?" I say, ever eloquent.

"On Saturday," he says, "I was wondering if, uh, maybe you wanted to get together?" I think that I really do like his shirt. I look up at him and say, "I'd love to."

9

(robert maguire)

Think about It, There Must Be Higher Love

Well, hello. I don't believe we've met. I'm Robert. Robert Maguire, that is. And I imagine by now you've heard a bit about me. You should probably know, right off the bat, that while a good deal has already been made about my Scottishness, I do not technically have a Scottish accent. Much like Carlie, a West Highland White Terrier hailing only historically from Scotland, I am American Scottish. I mention this because I thought it would be helpful for you to know what to expect linguistically, as I will be here on occasion, narrating. Narrating, offering my insights, call it whatever you'd like. What is important for you to know is that fictional characters are not without their insights. I myself have many.

Additionally, I feel it is important to point out that I

do not exist only within a children's-book universe. I also exist in the romantic realm. Ah, the realm of the romantic, what a place to exist. Because Amy thinks of me so very much, I've come to see that she conjures me before every date she goes on. She brings me to life every time she meets any man. She wishes those men could be me. Wherever she is, whomever she's with, she wishes on some level that I were there. And in a way, I am. To her, I am the perfect man. I love her dog. I understand her. I can read her thoughts, because I am one of them. And so I have decided to see what sort of insight I can provide, because after all I am so often with her, and I have come to see that I am quite important. And also, what else is there, actually, for me to do?

At the moment, Amy is getting ready to meet the man from the television studio. She is putting on lip gloss. She is not sure if this Saturday afternoon meeting actually constitutes a date. She ruminates on the phrasing of his invitation. "Do you want to get together?" "Do you want to get together?" has always been superior to "Let's hang out," but yet she reminds herself, lest she get too carried away, it has never held a candle to "Would you like to go out with me?" It could go either way, and she knows this.

Amy takes one last look in the mirror and heads to the kitchen, to Carlie's biscuit tin. Still, she wonders: date/not-a-date? It's a game she often finds herself playing in her single life in New York, because she is so frequently unsure of what anything actually means. I know I should refrain, but I cannot. If I exist only in the romantic realm, certainly it behooves me to be sure we stay within it. I steer her thinking just slightly in the direction of "date." Otherwise she may decide it's all platonic, may decide that he is far too sad and Lurch-like in his manner to be a date, that he wears too much eyeliner, or what have you. She'll get these thoughts in her head, these thoughts that there is nothing at all romantic going on. She'll move on to something else in her mind, some nonromantic pursuit, something that has nothing at all to do with one day finding love. And where will I be then? I really cannot say. Where do I exist if not in the romantic realm? I really do not know. And additionally, I must be vigilant to be sure that none of the men Amy meets ever manages to eclipse her affections for me. It has not yet come close to happening, but I remain ever on the alert. It's a tricky business. It is a fine line I must walk. I walk it well.

"Date," I whisper, and sometimes it's all so easy. I'm still here. Amy reaches into the biscuit tin and removes one of the beast's treats. Carlie looks up at her accusingly. Carlie appears to be concentrating hard on perfecting the facial expression she feels most properly relays, "You do a bad thing." I would shoo Carlie away if I could. It is my belief that Carlie employs this tactic because she is quite aware of its efficacy. She knows that on more than one occasion that look has in fact caused Amy to stay home. Sometimes I am sure that rascal knows absolutely everything.

Amy manages to resist *dear, sweet* Carlie's charms. She bends down and pets Carlie on her head. She tells her that she'll be back very soon and makes a swift and guilty exit. She closes the door behind her, and closes her eyes for a moment, too. She does this thinking that closing her eyes will somehow block the sound of Carlie's toenails on the wood floor, the sound of Carlie skittering after her to the door.

It doesn't work. She didn't think it would. Amy hears the sound of the toenails, and she pictures Carlie, even though she wishes she didn't, because it only makes matters worse. She pictures Carlie with the expression on her face that would best be described as *hmpf*, walking agitatedly around in that bowlegged way of hers, wondering how Amy could have left her, how this could have happened, yet again.

Amy tries her best to push the image of Carlie from her mind. I've felt her try to do this with me, with my image, at times. Sometimes she tries to get me out of her head. It causes me grave concern.

Amy reaches the bottom landing of the stairs, walks through the vestibule and out into the bright sun of the early afternoon. Nick is already out front, waiting for her, on time. He's facing the street and his back is to her, but it's easy enough to tell that it's him. He's dressed all in black and something about the angle and the brightness of the sun creates a slightly unsettling, but also in its way very appealing, halo effect. There is, in Amy's mind, only for the briefest of moments, the thought of an angel descending from heaven, of a cheesy, hokey soundtrack of angels singing as they look up at the light, and then she thinks of Ariel in *The Little Mermaid*, singing: *Ah ah ah! Ah ah ah! Ah ah ah!* Amy's mind does this, goes all willy-nilly and out of context too often; it does it more often than seems reasonable.

Nick senses her behind him. He senses her because he is off-course in his life. It is an oft-overlooked fact that being off-course in life can give a person heightened senses. He turns around, and even with the backlit effect, even with all the brightness, she can see that when he sees her standing there, he smiles. It's a big smile, a good smile, she thinks, one that isn't self-conscious, one that seems possibly real. I find it interesting that with all the things she can't see due to the subtle form of urban blindness she has now for so long been suffering, she can see his smile.

She shields her eyes as she walks up to him, and a bit awkwardly she extends her hand. "Hello. Nick," she says, two distinct, separate sentences. He doesn't seem flummoxed or even slightly thrown by the formality of her gesture, and she thinks how that's odd because she was herself slightly flummoxed, herself a bit thrown.

"Amy, hi," he says back to her. His greeting is all one

sentence, so much smoother than her effort. Once she gets closer to him, the halo effect goes away. And isn't it always the lack of distance that somehow erases the special effects? Isn't it always proximity that changes everything? I have to wonder if that could be why Amy is so careful to avoid it.

Amy lowers her hand, leaving her eyes free of any shielding. She sees that Nick's black T-shirt has the word *Sometimes* written across its front. Sometimes. She's sure that it must be more than just a word. She assumes it's a lyric, a song title, something from the eighties. She thinks it's from a song she should know, but doesn't.

"Hey," she says again, this time differently, wondering how many songs there must be whose lyrics she has forgotten, and whose lyrics she never knew in the first place.

"So," he says to her—the two of them such wordsmiths! He rubs his palms together quickly, as if it's cold out, as if it's not an unseasonably hot September day. "I was wondering if you wanted to take a walk around? The East Village is such a nice place to walk around, don't you think?"

"Yes," Amy says nodding her head, "I actually don't know it all that well."

"No? How long have you lived here?" Nick asks.

"Three years," she says, evenly, as if it's not an answer that exists only in the realm of the recluse. She thinks that maybe three years won't sound like a ridiculously long time to him, she thinks that maybe he'll understand.

He nods, though not very knowingly, she thinks. "So, where do you live?" she asks.

"Just up a bit, Stuyvesant Town. Do you know it?"

She pictures it, the jail-like complex over near the FDR Drive. She imagines it to be one of those places that everyone in New York knows about, so that her saying yes won't do anything to counteract the shut-in proclivities she has just now, perhaps too soon, revealed. But she nods, and says anyway, "Oh, yes," and adds in, "just up past Fourteenth Street, that complex." And with that they turn, and begin walking west. They pass 210 Fifth Street, which is a building that has a door that Amy likes very much. She admires it silently every time she passes. They walk up to Cooper Square before turning back on Sixth Street.

"So," she says, and I almost lose her again, as she goes off on some tangent in her mind about how she's always thought there to be something very interesting about awkwardness, about what causes it, why so many people are so often in its grasp.

Nick smiles down at her. It does not seem that Nick is going to say anything, not even a silence-filling "yeah," not "uh-huh," and so Amy looks ahead, not up at him any longer. She feels there would be something awkward in itself about looking up at him for any longer. "So," she repeats. "Eighties music? That's your thing?" And she thinks as she says it, in the moments before he answers, that the sentence came out not at all as she had planned.

"Yes," he says, "it is." She notes that he doesn't make any sarcastic or defensive quip in response to the fact that she just, albeit inadvertently, reduced his life's work to a "thing." She decides that this could mean he is kind. That, or very secure in himself, though because she suspects he's like her, she thinks that's not it.

"Not to say 'your thing,'" she clarifies, "as if it's just a hobby or something. I mean, I'm sure there's quite a lot of research involved, I'm sure it's quite scholarly." She hesitates. She wishes she could go backward in the conversation, as oftentimes in conversation she is wont to do. Why, she asks herself, did she have to bring attention to her conversational mishap, and why did she have to turn to the word *scholarly*? But then, as she looks back up at him, she sees his eyebrows rising, the corners of his mouth turning up. She sees from everything, the way his gait angles in a bit more to her, the way he smiles down at her, focused on her like a ray of light, that he's pleased. He is pleased at something she said, and she thinks it's the word *scholarly*, and she thinks, *Well, would you look at that.*

"It's interesting that you use the word *scholarly*."

Amy smiles up at him. Amy, I've found, is easy to read. I feel at times like these that were I not a fictional character, were I not only a product of her mind and thus so well equipped to read it, that I'd be able to read it anyway. Actually, I feel that anyone could.

"Yes?" she says, still looking up at him.

"Well, I do actually consider myself a musical scholar." He beams a bit as he says it, and the beaming, I think, is actually a bit rich. "My area of expertise," he continues, "is just one in which there has not yet been a lot of academic interest, so it's just, you know, *the eighties*, in this kind of campy way. I think the stuff that gets remembered tends to be the bad stuff. That happens. It happens all the time, if you think about it."

Amy nods solemnly in agreement. He speaks slowly, as if not only to make a point but also to clear up one that was made incorrectly. "I mean, there's so much. You've got your new wave and your synthpop, my personal favorites, and you've got everything else, too, right? Heavy metal, hip-hop, alternative, hard rock, lyrics, tunes, rhythms, all that. But what matters is that you've got this music, and this time, and you've got all these references, these songs that will forever play in the back of your mind, scoring all your most important moments," he says, gesturing with his hands.

"Yes, uh-huh?" Amy says. I think she's actually quite interested in whatever it is he's going on about.

"I mean think about it, all these songs, all these songs from when we were growing up, coming of age, our youth, whatever you want to call it. These are the songs that were first playing when our generation first started wanting things, and losing things, and hoping for things for ourselves. They were the songs that were playing when we first started dreaming things. They're our foot-notes." *So much to say,* I think, *and all at once.*

Amy looks up at him and smiles slowly. She thinks a bit longingly of the music of her youth. She thinks that maybe she didn't pay enough attention to it. She wonders if it's too late to start now. She'd like to find a footnote. She smiles at him again, or more accurately, she keeps smiling at him. She thinks she'd like to find a way to categorize her memories. And Nick apparently has more to say.

"I mean, the show, my show, yeah, it probably doesn't do everything it could in terms of seriousness, but it's hard to hold on to your vision, to do exactly what you want once so many people get involved," he explains. "It's hard to hold on to. I'm sure you're finding that out with your show," he says.

"Yes, I'll say," Amy says with a roll of her eyes. If only I were able to, I'd want to tell her never to roll her eyes. It's a gesture that has never once organized her features in a flattering way. "I'm also finding it hard to let go," she continues. "And I have a feeling that what I'm supposed to do at this stage is let go."

"No," he says, nodding, "I guess it's different." He looks down at her, and he doesn't smile, and there's a pause, a beat that Amy can almost hear, a drum being hit somewhere, in several places, in her past.

"But I know what you mean," she says. "I think I do

know something at this point about how hard it can be
to hold on to your vision."

"But, still," he says, the zeal fading out of his voice,
the molecules of passion almost visibly floating away. "I'd
also really like to do a full hour just on synthpop."

"Why don't you?" she asks.

"I don't know if anyone would watch," he says, smiling
down at her, a bit sadly. She looks up at him in almost
the exact same way.

They go into a coffee shop, he gets them both a coffee
to go. He asks about her books and she tells him about
Run, Carlie, Run! but not about the novel. They continue
walking together, mostly silently, an aimless serpentine
through the streets of her neighborhood, back and forth
from Avenue A to Cooper Square. Neither of them says,
"Let's go here," or "Let's go there," or "Let's make a plan,"
rather it's as if they've both silently signed up for the serpentine. She remains unsure as to if it's a date or not a
date. Strangely, there is something about that she likes.
There is something about *him* she likes. I wonder, if his
mind were the kind of mind that could be read, if I could
see there, written plain as day, that he liked it, too. I
wonder if I'd see that he liked her.

Occasionally as they walk, he stops to point things out
to her; he points out a shop that he tells her is his favorite haberdashery and she wonders, can one really have a
favorite haberdashery? How many can there be left? It's

called the Village Scandal and she likes the name and follows him in to look at the hats, to try a few on, to pose, and
she thinks right then that she is in the midst of a movie
montage. She is struck by the feeling that it is the type of
movie montage that is played when times turn tough. It's
the type of movie montage that is played to remind everyone that the characters used to be happy, and that they,
through all their current sadness, remember that.

A few blocks later, once they've crossed back and
are headed west, once she can see the tan brick façade
of *The Village Voice* in the distance, Nick points out a
gigantic looming structure to their right and tells her,
"That's the Ukrainian Chapel, it used to be hidden by
a building." A wave of his hand indicates the giant half-
block-sized hole behind a makeshift fence plastered with
advertisements for bands and albums, ones from this
decade. "And it will be again, but it's such a nice view of
it now, isn't it?" Amy is certain that the movie montage
has started to play again, and to tell you the truth, for a
moment there, it's as if I can see it, too.

She turns around, turns him around with her, and
they head back to Fifth Street. She brings him to her
door, not the plain glass, black-framed door of her own
hot-pink brick building, but to the door of Number 210,
the door she loves, the door she'd somehow like to call
her own. The building is stronger, bigger, both sturdier
and more elegant than her own. The door is beautiful,

grand, double-wide and covered with elaborate, detailed wrought iron; the design is plantlike, not quite floral. There's been something about this door that has held her interest from the first day she arrived here. It's been something she's thought about. She stands facing the door, a few paces away from it, and Nick stands next to her, their dissected reflections staring back from the pieces of glass between the wrought iron.

"I really like this door," she tells him. He's the only person she's ever showed it to.

He doesn't blurt out a response. He is not the snappy deliverer of lines that I am. He stares back at the door for a while. She watches his reflection. Something about it makes her feel close to him and something else about it makes her wonder for a moment if he's not real at all, if he's just a product of her imagination, too. And then he tells her how much he likes the door.

"Thanks," she says, looking up at him, squinting slightly in the sun before turning back to the door and their reflections in it.

After another moment, she says, "Nick?"

"Yes?"

"How did you first decide that your area of expertise was going to be the eighties?"

He hesitates again. And then after a while, he says, "Home."

"Home?"

"I moved around a lot as a kid," he says.

"Army brat?" she guesses.

"Well, kind of," he says. "Sort of more of a corporate brat. Though I figure we moved around about as much. In that sense, I never felt like I was *from* anywhere, you know? But the music was the only thing that ever stayed the same for me. It was the only thing I knew from place to place. Eventually I started to think of eighties music as where I come from. I still do."

She looks up at him. She nods slowly. And for a moment, I'm gone, for a moment she isn't thinking about me at all and I'm not with her. I'm not altogether sure what's happening. I only know it could be cause for deepest concern.

And then I'm back. And Amy and Nick are back at her actual door, the plain and unadorned one, the one she goes through every day. They say somewhat formal good-byes, and Amy thinks cautiously, always cautiously, that she felt something. It wasn't something blatant, nothing obvious like her heart skipping a bit. But then, she thinks her heart has perhaps already skipped enough. I noticed it, too. There was something small that happened, an almost imperceptible shifting of previously ignored molecules inside her. She watches Nick as he walks away, heading east, back in the direction from which I can only assume he came.

10

(amy)

You and Me Both

As it turns out, there is a clause in my contract that specifies that not only are Carlie and I committed for one year to *Things to Do in the City with Your Dog*, not only can I be, at any time, recast, but that also in the event of my recasting, I am legally bound to avail myself to the actress who will portray me in any way deemed necessary.

It is my belief that such a clause was put in place with the knowledge that I would be dispatched all too quickly. Renee says that such thinking is paranoid. Renee is not so high up on my "good" list. And so it is because of the clause much more than because I had, upon meeting Bonnie, recalled that I was a basically nice person, that I find myself staring down the very real possibility of spending every Sunday afternoon with Bonnie.

Bonnie, fresh-faced and scrubbed and long-limbed, thinks it imperative to her portrayal that she hang with me (her term, not mine), that she spend a really terrible amount of time with me (my term, not hers). Regardless of whether it has anything to do with the dog-friendly activities that will be explored on *Things to Do in the City with Your Dog*, Bonnie says she wants to see what my life is like. My life. As I sit at my desk with my laptop and she sprawls out on the carpet beside me, I almost don't have the heart to tell her that these days, I don't really have much of one.

Oh, and also, big bonus for me: now that Bonnie is here and now that I've spent a little bit of time with her, she doesn't quite seem as happy as she did when we first met at the studio. It no longer seems so incomprehensible that she, at some point in the not-so-distant past, struggled with depression, had an issue with mental health, or even, as they say not to say, had a nervous breakdown.

For the last three hours I have been sitting at my desk, staring at the empty Word document called *Swim, Carlie, Swim!* I have added the subheading: *Snake River (Wildest Wyoming)*. Bonnie has been beside me on the floor, arranging herself in a variety of yoga stretches, breathing deeply and occasionally chanting *Om*. Also, she has been talking to me about a person, who has yet to be named, who thus far has only been introduced as, "So there's this guy, right?" And she has been, over the course of the last several hours, deflating in front of my eyes. Or to be technically correct, this has been happening not in front of my eyes but out of the corners of them because I have been maintaining the pretense of "writing," which includes (and at this stage is also limited to) staring straight ahead at the computer screen. Bonnie's eyes are getting more and more shifty. I really can't imagine that any of this bodes well.

Bonnie sits up into a cross-legged position and stretches her arms over her head. When she reaches her arms over her head in a lean torso-accentuating cat stretch she reminds me of the cat-stretching Erin. I wonder if that's why Erin chose her to be me. I've heard it said that sometimes people dislike each other because they recognize their own negative traits within each other. So couldn't it be said just as easily then that exactly what draws people to each other is the recognition of the same positive traits? As Bonnie stretches herself out across my carpet, as Carlie swans around after her, I try not to think that if I were that pretty, that lithesome, if my legs were that long and my skin that glowing and fresh-scrubbed-looking, if I had translucent beauty down the way she does, I'd be happier.

"I just, I just don't understand why he wouldn't call, you know?"

I look down at her; I nod. I'd say it was about an hour ago that I first clued in to the fact that my participation in this conversation wasn't hugely needed. I had envisioned Bonnie walking around my apartment picking up objects and requesting gushingly that I share the story behind each one. I imagined her saying, "How does it *feel* to sit down to work on your book?" I'm not saying I'm not relieved that such is not the case. I'm just wondering if there couldn't have been some more agreeable alternative.

"No, really, I mean, do you know?" Bonnie asks me.

"Oh," I say. I pause for a moment and try to think of something to say. "No, I don't know, Bonnie," is the only thing I can think to say. And I have to say, I really don't know. I have to say I'm really the wrong person to ask when it comes to unearthing the intricacies of why people do what they do. I follow Bonnie's forlorn gaze, look along with her over at her enormous handbag, tossed recklessly on the floor. She sighs, and for an instant, I am almost completely overwhelmed by her moroseness. I have so far been unable to find an exit strategy, and so instead I do my part to keep the conversation going.

"What's his name?" I ask, and of course, as soon as I ask it, I worry it is the wrong question. It's probably not the best strategy to make "this guy" all the more real by reminding her of his name. As I've really meant to make clear, I am quite far away from being any sort of expert on matters of the heart.

"His name is Douglas. Was Douglas. Or is Douglas, I

can't be sure," she says, looking up at me doe-eyed, sor-rowful, the way Carlie might look at me were I to walk in and catch her gnawing on the Oriental rug. I am dis-tracted by Bonnie's concern over *is* and *was*. My first thought is, *Oh, look, Bonnie cares about verb tense, too.* I force myself to focus. I nod seriously.

"He hasn't called," she says, as if she's confiding a never-before-told secret, as if we haven't been on this topic already for quite some time. And then I feel old. I feel every one of my years. It's been so long since I was in my twenties, since I was young and in love—even if this love does seem to be a bit doomed—and waiting for someone to call me. Though, if memory serves, and in this case it does, waiting for someone to call is not the nicest feeling. So while I feel old, I feel safe, too.

"Okay, so there's a Douglas, and he hasn't called," I say slowly. I've always thought a good summary of events can be helpful. And I watch, slightly surprised, *dismayed* actually might be the better word, as Bonnie's eyes well up with tears. And still, I'm not quite sure how I signed up for any of this, if I signed up for any of this. I look over at Carlie, who is lying on her side, splayed out prostrate on the floor, looking glazed and slightly nervous herself.

"Yeah," Bonnie gulps, drawing my attention back toward her. She reaches into her backpack, removing a stack of index cards, three-by-five cards, clipped together with a black binder clip. Slowly, deliberately, she unclips the binder and tosses it carelessly back in the direction of her bag. She places the index cards down, directly in front of her feet in a perfect line with the place where one ankle crosses over the other. I think for a moment that we've moved on, that these cards have something to do with me.

"What are those?" I ask.

"My thoughts."

"On your portrayal of Amy?" I ask, because I have checked, and they decided not to go with Abilene.

She shakes her head no.

"I mean on your portrayal of Amie with an -ie?" I correct myself.

"No," she says, sighing deeply and nodding at the pile of cards. I follow her gaze and it's a pretty big pile of cards: fifty, sixty cards easily. "These are my thoughts on Douglas. Every one I've had since I last saw him." I don't say anything, I look down at the pile. Carlie gets up and hovers over the cards.

"You have to play the cards you've been dealt," Bonnie says, nodding seriously. I watch as she stacks the pile of cards in front of her, leaning over and banging the cards briskly on the floor to line everything up. She stares down at her stack, a momentary look of contentment crossing her face. She takes the top card off the stack and holds it in her hand, examining it for a moment, before carefully tearing off a corner. She places the torn corner in her mouth and after a pause, starts to chew. She places the card back onto the pile. She looks up at me, and she smiles.

Before I can do anything, before I can think of any way at all to react, before I can think too much about how much nicer yesterday was than today, Carlie jumps up and stares at the phone. This means it's going to ring, in about three seconds. My genius dog knows this. *Saved,* I think, *by the almost bell.* And then the phone rings.

"Hello," I say, picking it up on the first ring.

"Hi, Amy," I hear. "It's Lara."

"Hi, Lara," I say. Lara, who used to be my closest friend. Her husband is Jonathan's best friend; we did everything together. And now of course, we don't. And now, of course, Lara is no longer my closest friend. I don't think Lara and I really like each other anymore. But she's the only thing I have left from my old life, and mostly I try not to think too much about the fact that that's probably the only reason I'm unable to completely let her go.

"Well," she begins, "I've been looking at my calendar, and it's been a really long time since I've seen you. Of course, I'm sure a lot of that has been my fault since Chris and I have been out east all summer." By "out east" she means the Hamptons. I remember the Hamptons. "I mean, really, who is even in New York in September anymore?" she asks me. I don't answer, because the answer to her question would be, "Well, me," and also, "Everyone I know now," even though this is not an impressive number of people.

"But anyway," Lara continues, "we're back, some deal or something that Chris has, and I would just love if we could do something soon."

I grip the phone a little tighter, as if doing so will make me feel somehow less disconnected. It doesn't really help. I don't know why I thought it would; I've felt disconnected for as long as I can remember. When I lived in Colorado, I watched Woody Allen movies and listened to Broadway recordings. I imagined myself to be a New Yorker living in stealth disguise as a Coloradoan. When I lived on the Upper East Side, in Jonathan's world, I'd always had the nagging suspicion that I didn't belong there. I feel that way here, too, sitting in my apartment in the East Village, with my unwritten books and a depressive cable television host who's eating her index cards.

"Amy?"

"Oh, Lara. Sorry," I say quickly. "Right, absolutely. Let's get together soon."

"Lunch?" she says. Lara and I don't do dinner very much anymore.

"Sure," I say. "How about next weekend?" I suggest, realizing as I do that having not spoken to Lara recently, I have yet to tell her that I now have a new day job: former cable television host.

"That works. Want to say Sunday?"

Sunday, I think, looking down at Bonnie. I wonder if I make the lunch plan for Sunday if Bonnie will want to come, if I am in fact somehow contractually obligated to let her? Bonnie can't come, I think, standing firm on this at least. There must be boundaries and I must draw them.

"Sure," I say with slightly lowered voice. "Sunday sounds great."

As Lara and I say good-bye, with barely even a "How are you?" thrown in for good measure, I see that Bonnie has popped her head up from off the floor where she was resting it for most of the phone call and looks up at me expectantly.

"Bonnie," I say, slowly, calmly.

"You know, I've been meaning to tell you," she tells me, "you can call me Bon if you want. All my really good friends do."

"Okay, that's good to know," I say. "Next Sunday, I've actually got something I need to do. I need to see an old friend, and it's someone I haven't seen in a while, and I think it would just be all-around better if I went by myself." I explain this cautiously, uncertain how much control I'm allowed to have over my own life.

"That's fine," she says, to my great relief. "We can just do something Thursday night then instead? Do you watch *Grey's Anatomy*?" she inquires, instantly brightening. "Or we could even go out?"

I smile at her weakly. I nod at her perfunctorily. The words *new friend* run across the forefront of my mind like a lit-up marquee on the theatre of my thoughts. *New friend!* Except, I think, it's just the last thing on earth that I want.

II

(amy)

Show Me How You
Do That Trick

A dance floor, parquet wood and reminiscent of the 1970s, has been assembled in the center of the set. A grand disco ball hangs dizzily from the ceiling via an invisible wire, its girth partially obscuring the giant purple Carlie poster that hangs behind it. I wonder if there will be a strobe light. I myself have fallen somewhat out of character because I think it would be nice if there were. The episode that's being taped today is on dog dancing. Dancing, if you will, with your dog.

Carlie and Bonnie are on the set. There are more people here today, a cameraman, an assistant I've never met. I sit in my director's chair, the one that infuriatingly now says *Amie*, a ways behind the cameras and equipment and lights. I do this so that Carlie doesn't see me, so that I don't distract her, so that "the talent," as Barton has taken to calling her, does not lose focus. From where I sit, I can see that Bonnie appears to be having some trouble with her lines. It does not seem to be a day for her in which the happiness is being embraced; it actually doesn't seem to be a day for her in which happiness is even in the building. There is a part of me that understands. From my vantage point far across the room, I can also see that Bonnie has her hair curled in much tighter curls than the previous artful waves. I wonder if that's the gist of it, if that's all she took from our time together, that being me would be an undertaking best begun with curly hair.

Bonnie stares, doe-like, at the camera, and trips over another line. I'm not close enough to see but I feel that if I were, I'd see her knuckles turning white from holding on so tightly to the stack of index cards in her hands. It occurs to me that it could be the index cards themselves that are the problem, more of a problem even than they initially seemed to be. It occurs to me that Bonnie, in her rush to the stage, has grabbed the wrong set of index cards. She is up there beside the parquet dance floor, with Carlie on the seat next to her, without the talking points that Barton has written up for her on cavorting with your canine, but rather, with her index cards about Douglas, with her every thought about him since he last called her.

It's nerves, I think, she's nervous. Nerves can get the

better of a person even under the very best of circumstances. Clearly, these are not the best of circumstances.
I think how nerves might have an even bigger advantage
if they have, in the not-so-distant past, broken down.
I watch, nervous myself, as Bonnie tears at the corner
of an index card, and I feel something—what is it? Concern, protectiveness, friendship?—as I will her not to
remove the corner completely, and by all means, not to put
it into her mouth. I am not very good at willing people
to do things. I have to look away. I look over at Carlie
instead.

Carlie stares rapt at the camera, perched there on the
edge of her white leather settee, alert. It's as if she is but
moments away from lunging at the camera. I hope I am
correct in believing all the evidence that says she's fine
up there without me, because I don't think right now
that I can watch anymore. I get slowly up and out of my
director's chair. It isn't until I turn around that I realize
I've been sitting all this time not in my director's chair,
but in Carlie's. I head slowly to the soundstage door.

As I approach the door, I realize I must walk by
Erin, deep in conversation with someone else I haven't
met, right in the middle of my escape route. Though to
be technically correct, it is not an escape route at all,
because I don't get the overwhelming impression that
anyone assembled has particularly strong feelings about
whether I'm here or not. I walk less stealthily by them,

and neither Erin nor the unidentified person looks up. Sometimes I forget the level of my unimportance, and that's probably for the best. From the snippets of conversation that float my way, I learn there is some talk of Carlie appearing on a float in an upcoming Columbus Day parade.

"And since Columbus Day is a celebration of Italian heritage, maybe just for the day, we could call Carlie *Carla*, which sounds more Italian, doesn't it?" Erin suggests enthusiastically. "That would be really brilliant?" she adds. And I quicken my pace.

I wander through the hallway, up the length of it and back. I linger for a while outside the soundstage where they film *I Really Liked the Eighties a Lot*. And though I believe I am now too old to wait for someone's call, it's not as if I would have been unhappy had Nick called me. After a bit more lingering, and a bit more wandering, I find myself—*quelle coincidence!*—in the hallway just outside Nick's office.

I'm sure it's his office, from the eighties concert posters on the wall: The Cure, Erasure, Yaz, Depeche Mode, and one from a Flock of Seagulls concert. The door is open and I see a great deal of computer equipment, monitors and laptops, and speaker configurations, spread out across a large L-shaped desk. I look at the nameplate on the wall next to his door; unlike Erin's or Barton's nameplates, which have white lettering on a black background, the lettering on Nick's nameplate is electric turquoise.

"Hi, Amy," I hear, and I look up and there he is, right in front of me, and I try to act as if I'm surprised that I happened to run into him here, of all places. I try to act like this for his benefit, and also, I think, for my own.

"Hi, Nick," I say back.

"How's it going?" he asks.

I am almost compelled to tell him that it's not going so well, that I'm starting to see that sitting in any empty room trying to write the unwriteable *Swim, Carlie, Swim!* would be so much better. But, as I've learned, there is quite a difference between almost compelled and actually compelled.

"It's going great," I tell him, in lieu of the truth. I smile.

"Great," he says, smiling himself.

"How's it going with you?" I ask, after a blank pause and a bit more slightly awkward smiling.

"I can't complain," he says, and moves a bit past me, a step into his office, and then turns and says, "This is my office, by the way." I nod as if to say, *Oh, really? I had no idea.*

"Would you like to come in?" he asks. I stare up at his eyelinered eyes. He wasn't wearing eyeliner on the subway or when I saw him on Saturday. I don't know why I didn't notice that until now. I don't know what I think.

I don't know if I think that there would have been nothing difficult in asking me for my number, or if I should
go quite in the opposite direction and tell myself this is
silly, that he and I, we probably have next to nothing,
save for cable television, in common.

"Oh, no thanks, I should get back to the set," I say,
suddenly in a hurry, and as I do, I see for a moment past
the eyeliner, to his eyes. I remember that there is the
chance that we have things in common after all.

12

(robert maguire)

I Could Leave, but I Won't Go

Well, hello again. I sensed just moments ago that I would be back, and here I am. Here we all are, lingering outside Nick's office. Amy, it would seem, is not sure what she wants to do next. I don't really know either.

"Okay," Nick says, and Amy watches as he moves toward his desk. She turns as he pulls out one of those very ergonomically correct–looking chairs. As she starts to walk away, she hears him tapping randomly on his desk. Then music starts to play, something starting up mid-song.

The voice is deep, but the tune is light. The words float melodically to Amy's ears, to my ears, too. *Tell me what I've got to do, to make you notice, to make you look this way.* Amy's very next thought is, *I notice.*

Oh, I see what's happening here.

Suddenly, Amy is unsure if it was music she just heard, or if it was Nick. A big part of her is convinced it might have been Nick. Though another, equally big part of her thinks it could simply be that she has become a bit delusional in her latter years. Such a line of thinking concerns me.

She stops walking. She hesitates for a moment. If there is a moment to be had, Amy, more often than not, will find a way to fill it with hesitation.

"Nick?" she says, turning around.

He looks up at her, and as he does so, the goosenecked lamp that is clamped at an odd angle to the side of his desk catches the flecks of glitter embedded in his eyeliner. Amy does not care for the eyeliner. She tries to look away from the eyeliner. She tries to look at the man behind the eyeliner, mostly in order to discern if he looks surprised, if he spoke thinking she was already gone, thinking that she wouldn't hear him. I watch, a bit surprised myself, as she focuses first on his eyes, and zooms backward, panning out to include the rest of his features, his neck, his shoulders, the way he holds his hands. She doesn't think he looks surprised. "Did you just say something?" she asks him.

"Fine Young Cannibals," he says, and nods. He looks right at her, and then it is Amy who is surprised. Actually, I think she's more embarrassed than surprised as she meets his gaze. She feels a liquid warmth spreading through her, she thinks of ink spilled on a white tablecloth, escaping from a carelessly overturned ink bottle. Maybe this means she's going to write something? Of all the things it could mean, I'd like it to mean that.

"I'm sorry?" she says.

"Fine Young Cannibals." He says it again, pointing to one of his speakers with his pen. Her eyes fall on one of his monitors. On it a light show is pulsing to the beat of the song that is, after all, playing. "'Tell Me What,'" he adds.

"What?"

"The band, Fine Young Cannibals. The song, 'Tell Me What.' The fifth song on *The Raw and the Cooked*," he says matter-of-factly. "Good album," he concludes.

"Right, right," she says. She can't say for sure that what she wanted was for Nick to look up at her and say quite seriously, "Yes, Amy, I was just asking you what I had to do, to make you notice me." She can't say for sure what it was that she wanted him to say next. I can't either. But we both know that it was not "Fine Young Cannibals, 'Tell Me What' from *The Raw and the Cooked*."

"Nineteen eighty-eight," he tells her. She nods. "Look," he says, holding up a CD case. She stares at the cover, at the red and black squiggles outlined in white, a black-and-white photograph of a three-person band. He flips the CD case over and looks down at it, concentrating on it completely. Amy can't resist the thought that something in his expression, something fleeting, looks momentarily flustered. And I'd have to agree.

"Cool," she says next, I do not know why. Nick looks up at her and swivels slightly in his chair.

Amy wonders whatever happened to the Fine Young Cannibals. She imagines that if anyone would know, Nick would. And even though she knows it would please him to talk about it, she doesn't ask him. She only smiles. She only nods. I refrain from a tapping of the foot. The deep, disembodied voice, the one that is currently wafting out of the speakers, asks, "Is there something that I ought to know?" and Amy wonders where she was, what she was doing, the first time she heard this song, why she forgot all about this song, and all about the Fine Young Cannibals. She tries to remember.

"That's the album with the song 'Ever Fallen in Love with Someone You Shouldn't Have Fallen in Love With,' right?" she asks, and instantly, there's recognition in his eyes.

"That's it," he says, and then, "I hadn't pegged you as someone who was very up on eighties music."

Amy thinks that if they've made it this far without any revelations that her eighties had more to do with Debbie Gibson, Bon Jovi, and John Denver than with the bands that so preoccupy him, then there isn't any reason to provide such information at this juncture. I believe she could be right about that. "No, I'm not," she says. "But that was the big song on that album, right?"

"Well," Nick nods thoughtfully. "Sure, it got played a lot, and it's not like that album, at ten songs, is anything anyone would have called voluminous, nothing got lost on that album." He pauses. "But it's not like it was 'She Drives Me Crazy' or 'Good Thing,' which to my mind are what you would think of when you think of the big songs off that album. It's just, you know, kind of remark-worthy that you'd think of that song." He looks at her intently. She does not want it to be remark-worthy.

Because she does not wish to too deeply consider why it is that she blurted out, "Ever fallen in love with someone you shouldn't have fallen in love with?" and because Amy has found that grammar can be a wonderful tool for shifting the focus away from oneself, Amy looks back at Nick and says, "I think the word you want is *remarkable*."

"No, actually," he says, in a very pleasant tone, a nice voice, "the word I wanted was *remark-worthy*."

"Even though *remarkable* says the same thing, more efficiently?" she asks.

"Even though," he answers.

"Interesting," she says, pausing for a moment before asking, "Which song do you think of when you think of the album?"

"Me?" he asks, pausing to think for a moment. "I think

of track three. 'I'm Not the Man I Used to Be.'" He pauses again, looks right at her.

"I'm not the woman I used to be," she says without even thinking. It just pops out. This is new. He looks up at her intently. I am tempted to say he looks at her with understanding. But I am also tempted to keep that information to myself.

"No one is who he used to be," Nick says. "But that's not necessarily a bad thing."

Amy smiles. Nick smiles back at her. I think there may be something, perhaps a twinkle in his eye. And truth be told, there is a part of me that is not entirely sure this is a good thing.

And in the very next instant two other people are in the hallway, standing with Amy, right outside Nick's office. This isn't good either.

"Hi Erin, hi Barton," Amy says, and I can tell she doesn't want them here.

Nick swivels slightly away from them in his chair. He focuses on one of the monitors on the other side of his desk. These people, suddenly they're a part of this, it's the three of them, Amy and Erin and Barton in the hallway, and Nick is separate in his office. This is getting less and less romantic. I preferred it so much more the other way.

"Amy?" the one called Erin asks.

"Yes."

"We're a go for today?" she announces. Or asks. I find it so very hard to tell. "It was a really good day," she continues. "And I just wanted to let you know that next Tuesday, we're going to be on location? So, we'll be meeting at this really brilliant place in Chelsea that has a pool?"

"Okay," Amy says, and I feel myself fading away.

"It's going to be brilliant," the one called Barton chimes in. "We're going to have Bonnie in a purple bikini."

"The next episode is going to be called 'Doggie Swim'!?" Erin chimes back in. "It'll be really brilliant?"

"Swim?" Amy asks Erin, even though she heard her perfectly well the first time.

"Yes, swim?" Erin says.

Swim, Carlie, Swim! Amy thinks.

And I'm gone.

13

(amy)

Who Broke My Heart?
You Did, You Did

At the very end of a very long week I find myself uptown, just south of my old stomping grounds, at lunch with Lara.

"Please don't make me come down there," Lara had pleaded on the phone, when we'd talked again to firm up our plan. "What about Sarabeth's?" she suggested, and I knew she meant the Sarabeth's on Ninety-second Street and Madison Avenue, just a block away from her apartment and just a block away also from where I used to live.

"Fine," I said, "but Sarabeth's at the Whitney Museum, not the one all the way uptown."

"Okay," Lara had said, with a bit of martyrish sigh, believing that her journey eighteen blocks down meant we were in fact meeting halfway.

Once we've met in the cavernous lower level of the Whitney Museum, once we've been seated and ordered salads, and I've ordered a Bloody Mary, because to tell you the truth I just really can't make it through lunch with Lara without a cocktail anymore, I fill her in, somewhat reluctantly, on the details of *Things to Do in the City with Your Dog.*

"So wait," Lara says to me. "It's like a dog, on a TV show?"

"Well, it's my dog," I correct. "It's Carlie."

"And *Carlie's* the host? I'm sorry but I don't really get it. If Carlie's the host, is Carlie going to interview people? Or dogs? Will there be subtitles?" She peppers me with questions, and I think that my reluctance in telling her was most definitely justified.

"Well, yes," I say, speaking slowly, partially to be annoying, partially because I realize that if that last part was confusing, the next part is bound to be. "Carlie is the host, but there's also a person on the show, she's playing me, and she has all the speaking parts," I explain. Lara nods and furrows her brow, only the furrowing is all but imperceptible, due to Lara's fondness for Botox.

"So," she asks, the vision, for a moment, of concentration. "Who's Jimmy Kimmel in this scenario?"

"I don't think there really is a Jimmy Kimmel in this situation. But if there were, I think it would be Bonnie. Bonnie Beller. She's the actress who's playing me."

Lara looks up at me, cocks her head, blinks, and says, "Okay," and she nods once more, before briefly focusing most of her energy on pushing the beets off the top of her salad.

"So, if this person, Bonnie, plays you and Jimmy Kimmel, and Carlie plays Carlie, what do you do?" she asks after a moment. And really, I know that even though Lara may at times mean to be terrible, she doesn't mean to be terrible right now. Well, I don't know that, but for the sake of this lunch, that is what I tell myself.

I take a breath, a fortifying sip of my Bloody Mary.

"I take care of Carlie," I say, and Lara doesn't say anything.

After a moment, Lara looks back up from her salad and says, "Do you know I saw Missy Conner carrying a fake Goyard bag yesterday?"

"No," I say, focusing my own energies on my Bloody Mary.

"The fake ones are everywhere, it's a problem." The only reason I have any idea what she is talking about is that the last time I saw Lara, the time before this, she proudly showed me her new Goyard bag, only available at Bergdorf Goodman and Barney's, and explained to me that the real ones had monograms, and stripes. The fake ones did not.

I take another sip of my drink and I look back at Lara, all perfect outfit, all expertly matched accessories, and I think that I might finally need to put the shared history that Lara and I have aside. History, I'm starting to see, really should be aside. I look across the table at Lara. She is everything

I ran away from, everything I don't want to be around any-more. I wish—halfheartedly, yes, but still I wish it—that there were a way to explain this to her, to say, "Look, it's not personal, or rather, maybe it's a little bit personal, maybe if you were different, nicer, I could find a way to reconcile having you in my life, but you're not, and I can't."

And I know I'll never say that. And I wonder if, in lieu of that, we'll have no other choice but simply to drift apart further and further than we already have. I wonder sometimes what that will be like, if it'll be sad, if once she's gone completely from my life, if I'll miss her then. Or will it just happen so efficiently and effortlessly and seamlessly that neither of us, looking back, will have any idea what happened.

After a few minutes of silent salad pushing and silent Bloody Mary drinking, Lara looks back up at me, and I look at her and I notice her eyes have taken on a hint of panic.

"Amy," she says. "There's something I need to tell you." I hold her gaze, and I know that whatever she says next will be bad.

"Okay," I say, putting down my drink. I'm not even aware until I've already done it that I'm holding on to the table for support.

"Jonathan's getting married," she says quickly. *This is why she called me,* I think. Someone had to tell me. It should have been Jonathan. I hold on tighter to the table.

After a moment of complete blankness, I think that it's been three years. He's eligible, it's New York, land of the very many eligible women, and Jonathan is the marrying type. Of course he's getting married. I am fine with this, I tell myself, draining my drink. And if I'm not fine with this, I also tell myself, it will not be revealed in front of Lara.

"It's okay," I say, nodding slowly. I feel that if I nod slowly, if I speak slowly, the fact that I say it's okay will somehow seem truer. "I'm fine."

"Are you sure?" Lara asks me.

"I'm sure," I say.

"Because you don't look fine, you look sad."

"I'm not sad," I say.

And next, in a genuine but perhaps misguided effort to make me feel less sad, Lara offers up, "Well if you are, don't be. Really. I mean sometimes I wondered what you even saw in him anyway."

I nod. I've wondered that, too. I've wondered for a long time what I had seen in Jonathan, and also, what he had seen in me. I've gone back and forth and back again, and now for the first time, I realize what it was. When I met Jonathan, everything about him said "sophisticated New Yorker" to me, and everything about me said "young" and "carefree" and "from somewhere far away from here" to him. It's only right now that I realize that what attracted us to each other were the very things that we weren't, the things that seemed at the time just out of our reach.

"It's fine," I say again, this time with a bit more authenticity. "I'm okay," I say, and it occurs to me that maybe I am.

"You are?" Lara asks, seeming almost truly relieved that I am. As she reaches across the table and touches my arm, I think that I should at least consider taking back all the things I just thought about not being friends with her anymore.

"I am."

"That's really good, Amy," she says, moving her hand from my lower arm to my wrist. "Because there's something else."

I look up. Her fingers move lightly from my wrist to the back of my hand. I don't say anything.

"Gwen?" Lara says next, and I am momentarily confused. "Jonathan's fiancée?" she clarifies, and I think for a moment that I don't really mind hearing that phrase, and isn't that a good thing, isn't that a step in the right direction. I wait. "She's pregnant."

I stare back at Lara. She looks at me with panicky eyes. She breathes in again. I grip the table for support. I don't think there will actually be any support in the table, I don't imagine it will have any solidity or even any stability, let alone support. But right now, here, I don't think I could think of a source of sufficient support. So I imagine the table, as insufficient and made out of Silly Putty as it could very well turn out to be, is as good a bet as any.

"Maybe," I say, "we could talk about something else."

14

(amy)

Don't Say a Prayer for Me Now

can't think about it. I really can't.

I'm not thinking about it, and I can tell myself I'm fine. If I think about it, it's entirely possible I won't be able to. Though it's not something I have often practiced, not thinking about things can be very good. It can be an elixir to a great many problems if you let it. Really, it can.

Over the course of the week, I have done my best. Not. To. Think. About. It. Carlie has had a swimming lesson in Chelsea, has run an agility course in Park Slope, and has gotten into a bit of a tussle with an Airedale at a dog run in Riverside Park. With all this on-location time away from the studio, I have seen far too much of Erin, and almost nothing at all of Nick. And now that it's once again Sunday, Bonnie is once again here, camped out in my living room. She's been here all day, while I have *really been meaning to write*, but have not *actually been writing*. Bonnie shows no signs of leaving. Though that doesn't say anything for certain. She did at one point earlier wander aimlessly away, returning an hour later with a tuna roll, which she deposited in my refrigerator, and with a giant-sized Arizona iced tea, which she has taken with her to the carpet. Her index cards have been, and remain, arranged in a semicircle around her.

While I pretend to stare only at the blank white page of my computer screen, I watch her out of the corner of my eye. I see her place the index card she's been holding, and yes, also snacking on, down. I see her reach one of her long arms over to one of the lower shelves of the bookcase. She leans back and pulls out a long, thin book. I know, of course, without even seeing the cover that it's one of the first editions of *Run, Carlie, Run!* when Carlie and Robert Maguire were in Scotland, long before there was even the thought that they might visit Paris or the Congo, long before Carlie and Robert Maguire felt the call to Wyoming and a white-water raft. Or kayak, who even knows anymore. I watch as Bonnie runs her hands across the embossing on the cover, the raised design elements next to the smooth renditions of an illustrated Carlie and an illustrated Robert Maguire. I forget that I don't have to differentiate between an illustrated Robert Maguire and a real one, the way I do with Carlie, because—and how can it be said without also saying the word *alas*—they are one and the same.

I look down at Carlie, the real Carlie, resting with her chin up on one of Bonnie's cross-legged thighs. Bonnie opens the book, and I watch as a slow smile spreads across her face, and for a moment I am free. For a moment I don't care about what it is that I am "supposed" to be writing. I don't care at all about properly constructed sentences or literary acclaim. For a moment, however fleeting, I think that this, here, the ability to make someone smile, to make someone put down her index cards, each one a slice of heartbreak, and because of something I've done, smile, is important.

"The Carlie books?" she begins, looking up at me. "The *Run, Carlie, Run!* books? That's what they're called, right?"

"Right," I say and I wonder if she knew I'd been watching her, instead of her watching me, as was the original plan.

"They're so good. That must make you so happy."

I nod my head and think that yes, that book right there, with the Snake River not even a thought in Carlie's and Robert Maguire's minds, it does.

"Yes, it does make me happy," I say. "Happy can be tricky though, you know?" I add on, not even thinking she's really listening, but she perks up quite a lot at my last sentence. She looks at me, eyes wide.

"Yes," she says, nodding sagely. "I know that." She gets up slowly and walks to the kitchen and returns with the foil container of sushi. "Do you want some?" she asks me.

"Thanks, no," I say.

"Right," she says as she places the tuna roll on the coffee table and sits down again on the floor, bringing her hand to her mouth and poking distractedly at her lip. I watch, no longer even the slightest bit shocked, but still, I have to admit, a bit fascinated as she looks in front of her, at one of the several piles of index cards around her, and randomly selects one. She absentmindedly tears a small section of the index card off. I notice that she tears off the section of index card carefully so as not to interfere with any of the text. She doesn't want to lose any of her writings on Douglas. She folds the torn-off piece of index card over onto itself and puts it in her mouth, and begins to chew, slowly, her mouth closed. I want to say, "What about the tuna roll? Why not eat that?" But I don't.

"So, you know," she says, "about Douglas?" As she says it, my gaze lands again on the blank white screen, and I get anxious, because of the writer's block, and if I'm completely honest about it, because I'm not as nice as I'd like to be and I think I've already talked more than any person can reasonably be expected to talk about Douglas. I don't want to talk about Douglas anymore, not ever.

"You know, Bonnie," I say, maybe a little impatiently,

but for the most part, as nicely as I can. "I need to do a little work right now. If I don't get some words down pretty soon, I might have a nervous breakdown," I say, and then I think, *Oh. Oh, damn. Oh, damn, oh, damn, oh, damn.*

"Nervous breakdown?" Bonnie says, suddenly even more focused, fixing me completely in her gaze, a gaze that strikes me as serene and knowing and calm, a wise old gaze. It's an unsettling look coming from a person currently more famous for having a nervous breakdown than she is for anything else.

Oh, I think, *not good.*

I should not, not under any circumstances, refer to nervous breakdowns. I notice how truly upright and flawless Bonnie's posture is as she sits cross-legged on my floor, Carlie's chin once again resting on her thigh. Carlie is looking up at Bonnie soulfully, in the hopes of receiving a section of tuna roll. Bonnie is looking up at me calmly. I question everything. Why has she lost interest in the tuna roll? Why did I say that about having a nervous breakdown? Why is this my life?

Bonnie takes a deep breath, inhaling slowly through her nose. I watch her, wondering if this is what would constitute a deep, cleansing breath. One can hope. She closes her eyes. Ever the burgeoning optimist I would so like to be, I wonder if she closes her eyes in an effort to find her spiritual center. She opens her eyes and looks back at me. Carlie still practices her subtle manipulations in hopes of the tuna roll. I wish she wouldn't.

"Carlie," I say. There is no reaction, no indication from anyone in the room that I have spoken.

"Nervous breakdowns," Bonnie says again, still calm. I can't help but wonder if the calm might be the type that could best be described as eerie. "I think nervous breakdowns are everywhere, really. I think they're like molecules, these tiny invisible things floating through the air, just waiting, just looking for the right person to happen to. Sometimes I think it's all just a matter of time."

Bonnie and I look right at each other. I don't know how long we sit there looking at each other, I only suspect that it feels like much longer than it actually is. I feel so connected to her. And then I feel on the verge of being overwhelmed with anxiety. I eye Bonnie's pile of index cards. Really, I do. And then Carlie runs to the front door, and stands underneath the buzzer barking at it, and a second later, it buzzes. It's so unlike me, but I think no matter who may be downstairs buzzing, it's really very nice that they're here.

"It's Renee Van!" comes through the intercom. I buzz her in. It's not completely weird for my agent to be here on a Sunday since she goes to Pilates in the East Village on Sunday evenings; every now and again she stops by when she is in friendlike agent mode. Also, I imagine

Renee is trying to be pal-zy with me, because of the contracts, because of the clauses, because in her efforts to
further and foster my career, she has really only furthered
and fostered the career of my dog. She knows that lately
I'm a lot more than a little annoyed with her. I would
imagine she knows I've even thought about looking for
another agent. The only thing that prevents me is that I
don't have any books currently being written for anyone,
Renee or not Renee, to represent. As I go to the door and
stand by it with Carlie, as I listen to Renee clomping up
the stairs, I resolve not to let on how very welcome her
visit is at this particular juncture.

"Hi, Amy!" Renee says as she arrives at the top of the
stairs and teeters in wearing spandex exercise leggings
and very high platform wedges. "Michael Kors," she
informs me when my gaze lingers too long upon them.
"Hi, Bonnie," she adds with a syrupy tone to her voice as
she positions herself on the couch. Carlie barks at her.

"Hi, Renee," Bonnie says sweetly from the floor.
"Would you like a cup of herbal tea?"

"Oh, thanks, Bonnie, that would be lovely," Renee
answers looking pleased, and then less so, as Bonnie gets
up, walks with the tuna roll into the kitchen, and then
returns to her spot on the floor empty-handed. As Renee
sits quietly on the couch, tea-less, regarding Bonnie on
the floor, without launching into any explanation of why
she's here, it occurs to me that maybe she doesn't have a

reason. Maybe even Renee feels a little bit alone on Sunday evenings, too.

"Okay, Amy," she says next. "The reason I'm here?" Or then, I think, maybe not.

"Uh-huh?" I say.

"I've set up drinks for you with a friend of mine, Tom Gruen. He's a brilliant editor over at Argonaut Press. He edits very important literary fiction."

"Because of my novel?" I ask, confused, because Renee doesn't very often pay attention to my novel, and also, because as I believe may have been mentioned, my novel has yet to be written. The only editor Renee ever mentions to me is Victoria, the editor of the Carlie books, and that's usually in the same sentence lately as the words, "She's waiting." Renee just looks at me sweetly. It doesn't suit her.

"Well, not exactly because of your novel, *per se*," she smiles.

"Are you setting me up on a date, Renee?" I ask.

"Why don't you just look at it as drinks? Why does everything have to have a label?" she asks me breezily, waving a hand in the air. "See if it goes anywhere. Either way, he's a really nice person to know." I think that I don't want to push the point, because I don't like talking about dates with Renee, and also because I don't really want to draw any further attention to the fact that I have become a bit confused, if you will, about romance in recent years. I think to myself that he's an editor of great literary novels. Maybe just meeting him will help with my writer's block. Only, with Nick, with all the recent ambiguity that I at least like to *think* is there, I don't know if I'm really up for another round of date/not-a-date, which is a game I feel I so often play. No, I think, I don't think I'm up for another round.

"Renee," I say, "I don't really think I'm up for it right now. I've got a lot going on at the moment, and who has the energy? Who has the time?" I ask, trying for breezy, too, but falling sadly short.

Renee looks over at me, blinking slowly as if to say, *Wrong answer.*

"Amy," she says firmly, "you have the energy, you have the time," as if every time I've listened to her it's worked out so well. Months ago I would have agreed, whole-heartedly even. I would have said that, yes, every time I listened to Renee it worked out smashingly, swimmingly, dashingly. But now, as my gaze falls warily on the floor in front of me, piled high with shredded index cards, Bonnie sprawled across it, fingering a script, the large bold capital letters THINGS TO DO IN THE CITY WITH YOUR DOG printed glaringly across it, I can see now that is no longer the case.

"Amy," she says again, and I look away from the floor, the cards, the script, my constant forced contemplation of my alter ego; I look up, directly at Renee.

"Yes?" I say.

"You should go, get out a bit." Normally I would tell her

that I'd be perfectly happy if I never left the house again. But when was the last time anything was normal? When could that have been? I look around again at the scene that surrounds me, and I think that Renee, though wrong, may be right. And also, getting out might just help me not to think, about those things I really need not to think about.

"You should meet him," she tells me. "It's a good connection for you, either way. Connections are important," she adds.

I nod my head. I say, "All right. I'll go."

"Okay then," Renee says, smiling wildly, broadly, perhaps falsely. "It's a plan."

But, I think, *is it a date?* And I think of Nick, who might have my number, so to speak, but has not yet tried to dial it, so to speak, and I realize that I'm pretty sure I don't want it to be. A date, that is.

As Renee leaves, teetering on her wedge shoes, Bonnie takes a long sip from her giant iced tea through her straw and watches her go. I notice that nothing moves but the focus of her gaze, following Renee as if her eyes are attempting to jump over her eyebrows. And as her gaze escorts Renee out of the apartment, as her eyes linger on the door, while she never even stops sipping from her straw, it occurs to me how very very much Bonnie notices. I wonder if any of this, if any of anything I do, will wind up being caught and transferred to film.

(robert maguire)

You Could Meet Someone Who Really Loves You

Amy is sitting on the floor in the bedroom, looking in the mirror that hangs on the back of the closet door, putting on mascara. As this is an act that Carlie has come to associate with Amy's going out without her, Carlie, in the hopes of getting Amy to reconsider such a plan, is lying by the front door, on her back, proudly displaying her belly. While I can't be sure of her logic, I believe Carlie displays her belly in this way because, sometimes, it is quite effective. Sometimes Amy will drop whatever she is doing and say, "Oh, the belly!" And then she will drop down to her knees to reverentially rub the belly. I suspect at times that Amy is misguided, and I believe this nonsense with the belly to be a perfect example of such a loss of direction.

In fairness to the little beast, how could Carlie, who can never quite grasp the fact that the world doesn't revolve around her, really ever be expected to accept anything less? It is, in my humble opinion, a problem. Especially because Carlie, there, belly displayed for all the world to see, is only setting herself up for disappointment. For as sure as she's applying mascara right now, seated cross-legged in front of the closet door mirror, closet door ajar, because the lighting in the bathroom has never been any good, Amy is on her way out.

She inserts the black mascara wand back into its tube and twists it shut. She tosses it back into her wicker basket. Amy keeps all of her makeup collected in an old wicker basket that has been painted a color one might be inclined to call maroon. Its origins are a mystery. She likes to think it is from Pier One but sometimes she worries it is an antique basket brought with her accidentally from Jonathan's. As she rummages through it for her blush, she hopes she never knows for sure. If it turned out to be an antique basket, procured perhaps at an Americana auction at Sotheby's, she is sure she'd have to get rid of it. And if she were going to accidentally take things from Jonathan, she can think of things she'd want more.

She stares at herself in the mirror for a moment, before sliding the basket, along with an orange coffee mug in which she keeps her collection of makeup brushes, packed in with a few lip gloss wands, over toward the side wall of the closet. She gets up and steps into her shoes, bends down to buckle a strap around one ankle and then the other, and shuts the closet door. Carlie is still on her back, still on her crusade. Her legs are still splayed above her and out to the side. Carlie stares straight ahead, eyes almost glazed, beadlike, as if she is certain that if she musters enough concentration she can will Amy's departure away. Though I can't say for sure, because I can't read Carlie's mind. Well, that's not entirely true; every so often I can read it, just never nearly as well as I can read Amy's.

Amy, no expert at moving forward, is caught up in her mind as she walks through the apartment. She thinks of me; she so often thinks of me. She has thought of Jonathan now, by way of the wicker basket. And she has, in a way I think altogether inappropriate, thought of the character from the television studio, Nick. Her progress is slow through the short length of the apartment. Her progress, it could be said in reference to many things, is generally slow.

Amy approaches the front door at last. Carlie stares with great intensity as she comes closer. Right before she reaches Carlie, Amy makes a quick turn to the left, into the tiny square of her kitchen. She reaches into a cream-colored stoneware canister and removes one of Carlie's biscuits. And, Carlie, in spite of her best efforts to remain vigilant, finds herself distracted by the siren song of the biscuit. She gets up from her belly-displaying blocking of the door and takes the treat from Amy. She is shocked, indignant, as Amy slips quickly through the door.

Amy shuts the door softly behind her. As she turns her key in the lock, as she listens for the sound of Carlie's toenails on the floor skittering to the door, she makes a concerted effort to move, at least physically, forward.

She turns and walks determinedly down the stairs, through the vestibule, and out onto the street. She does not look both ways before she crosses. She makes a pact with herself, or rather I think it's more of a promise to herself. She will live, she tells herself, in the moment. She will not think about Jonathan, about engaged-and-expecting-a-child Jonathan. She will not, she tells herself, think about the strange yet compelling man, Nick. Well, I should think not. As her feet travel slowly, and then more briskly, picking up speed with each step across Fifth Street, the stretch of pavement that she has for so long endeavored to think of as her own, she resolves with an almost imperceptible shake of her head not to think of either of them.

She tries, with a certain degree of earnestness, a great deal more than could actually be called characteristic of her, to think only of what's in front of her. She tries to think about her date, or her professional meeting, which-ever it may be. She walks on. She needs, she thinks, to stop thinking so much about so many other things.

She turns at the corner, heading briskly in the direction of Astor Place and the subway entrance there. I do love the entrance to the subway on Astor Place. There's something about it that I find to be both cinematic and rather European. And then, and oh, I do suppose I should have seen this coming. I should have seen this on the proverbial horizon as something quite inevitable, as a conclusion quite foregone: Amy resolves not to think of me either. It had always been my understanding that I existed firmly in the romantic realm, that whenever anything came up that was even the slightest bit connected to the promise of love, I would be there. I used to be. I'd be there because what mattered was that I was the perfect man for her. I am the perfect man. I am the only man for her. I am the only man she really wants. Yet lately, that seems less and less to be the case. Lately, it does seem that at times she wishes to forget me. And worse yet, far worse yet, there are times she does not want me at all. I listen, unable to stop it, as she resolves once again not to think of me. I can only hope that such a resolution will only be for a night, or perhaps for not even as long as that. I can feel myself holding on, holding on to the belief that such a thought, such a resolve, can be only fleeting.

And then I'm gone.

16

(amy)

Desperate but Not Serious

I am at the giant, curving structure of the Time Warner Center. Or I am at The Shops at Columbus Circle. I'm not sure what the place is technically called; sometimes, it gets hard for me to keep up. I'm up on the third floor, at Café Gray, seated at the bar, waiting.

"It's Tom!" he says loudly from across the room as he enters. He approaches, tall and dark, with somewhat wild hair, and notably crazy eyes. He's wearing a solid black rumpled suit over a striped shirt undone a few buttons from the collar, no tie. I reach out for his slightly doughy hand.

"Hi, Tom," I say. He leans in and envelops me in a strong bear hug. He smells like cigarette smoke. He pulls back and stares at my face for a moment before leaning back in and kissing me on the cheek.

"You must be Amy," he says. I am so tempted to say no.

"Yes, hi," I say instead.

"I hope you weren't waiting long."

"No," I say, "not at all."

He eyes the empty bar stool next to me, and then looks across the bar to an empty banquette table. He motions back to it with a flick of his wrist. "Do you want to see if we can get that table?" he asks me.

I agree with him, "Sure."

The host is agreeable: it's fine for us to take the table, we've met here fairly early in the evening, and the barroom is not yet crowded. We're led to the small round table right by the entrance, and we sit together, side by side, on the banquette. Tom leans back against the black leather cushion and stretches a long leg out into the aisle. He hoists his other foot up onto the empty chair on the other side of the table. The host returns, less agreeable, to shake his head at Tom, and then, perhaps as a reprimand, he takes the chair, in its entirety, away. We order wine, and make only the smallest of small talk as we wait for it to arrive. I've made such an effort already not to think about so many other things that I feel I'm almost asking too much of myself to avoid pondering the date/not-a-date qualities of the evening. I try, though. I try just living in the moment.

The wine arrives. We toast the fact that it's nice to

meet each other, though personally I believe the jury to be still out. He stares at me intently.

"So, you're an editor at Argonaut Press?" I say.

"Yes," he says smiling, nodding authoritatively.

"How long have you been there?" I inquire.

"Eight years," he tells me, staring at me, leaning closer.

"Eight years is a long time in publishing, from what I hear," I say, a bit lamely. "You must be happy there."

"Oh, I am," he says. "I mean, it's corporate and I work for the man, but it's a good place to be, and we publish some great books." I am not sure how exactly this leads to Tom's flipping over one of the cardboard Café Gray coasters and drawing me a diagram illustrating his philosophies on getting ahead as an editor, a pie chart of sorts of the exact combination of talent, work ethic, and longevity that is essential, but somehow it does. I follow the diagram and nod. I say how interesting it all is. I feel offput by both the glaring intensity of his eyes and the strong smell of stale cigarette smoke coming from his clothes.

"And you?" he asks, after converting the pie chart into a bar graph. "Renee tells me that you write children's books. I don't know very much about the genre, but please enlighten me," he says with a crooked smile, and, *oh no*, I think I feel a hand on my knee. I move back ever so slightly; the hand doesn't follow. "Tell me about your books," he says, with a spark in his eye.

"They're called *Run, Carlie, Run!*" I say. "They're about the adventures of a West Highland White Terrier named Carlie and a Scottish explorer named Robert Maguire." I remind myself sternly that I am not, for the purposes of this evening, permitting myself to think how much nicer it would be if I were here with Robert Maguire instead. And actually, I think it wouldn't be half bad to be here with Nick. Except I'm not thinking about that either.

Tom does not seem interested in my books, though his hand returns to my knee.

"So," he says next, a bit heavily, "I gather you have a dog?" There's something in his eyes that seems to say that when my answer is yes, he will disapprove.

It's not that I don't want to talk about my dog. Of course I want to talk about my dog—if you look at it from a creative standpoint it's really all I do—but if I've learned anything over the years I have spent devoted to Carlie, I've learned that not everyone loves to discuss in great detail what I perceive to be the inner life of my dog.

"Yes," I say. "Her name is Carlie," I add, aware that I am again perhaps stating the obvious.

He nods, and says, "Uh-huh," in a way that to me seems to say, *I knew it!*

I turn to him, a bit miffed, and say, "What?"

"No, nothing," he says, leaning back, removing his hand from my knee and signaling for the waitress. For a

moment I think he's just going to ask for the check, and
I think I don't mind, and I think I don't like him either,
and at least he's honest. Then he turns to me and indicates my half-empty wineglass, and asks, "Another?"

Honestly, I'd rather say no, but I am not so honest, so
I nod my head and say, "Yes, thanks."

As we wait for our wine, he turns back toward me,
to face me, to fix me again in his smothering gaze. His
hand returns, as if drawn by magnet, to my knee.

"It's just this whole thing going on, in New York,"
he explains, "with women and their little dogs. It's like
they're all their foster children."

I look at him for what feels like a full minute, straight
on. I wish I had done this a moment ago, so I could have
recorded his features, remembered what he looked like,
how different he must have seemed then, when I thought
of him as just a bit smug, wild-haired and crazy-eyed, and
a bit too impressed with himself, in the seconds before
I decided he was a terrible person. But it's too late, that
time has passed.

"I think what you must mean is *surrogate child*. And I
don't think that's really an accurate description. I don't
think that's how women see their dogs."

"No," he says, raising both his eyebrows. "I mean foster children. And I'm pretty sure, last time I checked,
that all single women in the city have this thing going on
with their little dogs."

I don't like this. I don't like the way he is referring to Carlie as a little dog. Maybe he'd think differently if he'd read just one example of the *Run, Carlie, Run!* oeuvre. Carlie is an international traveler, an adventurer, an averter of the darkest disasters. Suddenly, I picture this man, this Argonaut Press editor, looking very much as he does now, only his face is green, only he wears a pointy hat, only he straddles a broomstick and he is tilting his head back and shouting maniacally into the whipping wind, "I'll get you, and your little dog, too!"

Then, just as suddenly, that image is replaced by the thought that I do—regardless of genre, regardless of whether there is the stamp of the Argonaut Press logo (a very nice sailing ship, by the way) on its spine—I do have an oeuvre. Oeuvre. A body of work. I linger for a moment on the thought of how that would sound if I said it out loud: "I have an oeuvre." And as I do, it occurs to me that the reverence I have always had for certain things may be misplaced.

"I just don't see how you can make such sweeping generalizations," I say, and his eyes are sharp, intelligent, even though I wish I could say otherwise.

"I don't see how you can see it any other way," he answers back quickly, and it is his persistence as much as it is his subject matter that makes me think he answers back meanly, too. "I mean, to guys at least, women in their thirties, I mean maybe not early thirties, but say, thirty-four and up," he says and pauses, checking some kind of internal record of women he's known. "These women, everywhere, it's so obvious, they want to have kids, they wish they had kids, and so they get these little dogs and they talk to them like babies, carry them all over the place in designer bags, dressing them up. It's so blatant, really, is what it is."

Carlie never dresses, I think indignantly to myself. And she hates her bag with the power of a thousand suns. In my mind, I am slamming a flattened palm down on the table for emphasis. In reality, in lieu of that, I stare at him with narrowed eyes. *Run,* I think, *Amy, run!*

"Still," I continue, in spite of myself. "What you're saying, it's a generalization. I mean, consider this: I have Carlie, and yes, I love Carlie, but it's not as if I have her because I really want a child, because I'm not even altogether sure I want to have kids." The words are out of my mouth, and I don't even know if I'm just making a point, or if I actually mean it. Tom Gruen is looking at me with just the slightest tilt of his head. Wait. The very reason Jonathan and I drove to Cape May, New Jersey, to get Carlie was because I was in my early thirties and wanted a baby, and because I wasn't going to have one, not in the marriage I was in, which at the time had yet to become one I could conceive of ending. I am aware that *conceive* is actually a very poor word choice at this juncture.

"You don't really think that," Tom says, giving me an out. "No one thinks that." And I think that maybe I do. Only I don't know. It's just so new. It's just I've never said it before. "No one thinks that," he says again, as if he hadn't already said it quite clearly, as if I'd chosen not to hear him. And as he says it, the one thing I'm thinking is that he can't be right. A man like this can't be right.

Instinctively, I look down at the floor. I do this because I'm so used to seeing Carlie there when I do. I don't know if I think of her as my child. How would I know, not having ever had one? I think of the TV show, of the inordinate amount of time I have spent sitting in a director's chair with my incorrectly spelled name written across it, next to a director's chair with *Carlie* spelled out across it. I think of how many of my days are spent waiting for Carlie to finish her day under the pretense that I wait for that so that I can begin mine. The truth is that my day has become her day. The things I have to do have become the things that Carlie has to do. I don't think I ever set out to think of Carlie as my child, but yet here I am, undeniably a stage mom.

Our second glasses of wine arrive, and as much as I need a drink right now, I don't think I can drink it. Tom's hand returns to my knee. I look down at my wrist.

I'm not even wearing a watch, my watch is broken, but I think that's a tiny detail, a nothing detail.

"Tom," I say looking back up, compelling myself to speak slowly and carefully, to convey an air of calm, even if I in no way possess it, even if in my mind I am already running out the door. "It was really a pleasure to meet you. But I actually have to go now. May I give you some money to pay for my portion of the bill? And do you think you could take your hand off my knee?"

"Oh," he says, looking not even the tiniest bit flustered. "If you want to hang out for a minute, we can share a cab downtown? Renee told me you live in my neighborhood?"

"Oh," I say, "no. I'm heading somewhere else," and as I say it, I realize I am gesturing to the left, which geographically, I think, is west. Tom declines my offer for cash, and thankfully remains to drink more wine. I say good-bye, and I somehow refrain from saying, "Screw you and the horse you rode in on," and I dash out the door.

I am at a run en route to the escalator. Once I reach it, it's crowded with people, half of whom are not standing off to the right side as they are supposed to, so unfortunately, I must stand. I try to take deep breaths as I am led mechanically away.

As I descend to the second floor, I see the wide and

gaping entrance of the Borders bookstore there. I walk, more calmly, into the bookstore. It will be safer here. I stand for a moment, just inside the entrance, taking it all in. For me, there used to be nothing like a bookstore. It's changed recently, with the writer's block, with the novel, Great American or otherwise, that may never be written, with the fact that every book on the *New!* table, there in the *Favorites!* section, there on the *Fiction!* display has become a small reminder of what I might never do.

Straight ahead of me there is a red sign with white lettering. The sign reads *Events* and there's an arrow pointing left. I turn left. As much as I sometimes think it would suit me to be a rebel, there lives within me an inherent rules-follower. And also, I don't know what else to do.

There is, as it turns out, no event. But there are rows and rows of chairs set up and there is a podium at the front, as if a reading is about to take place. I take a seat a few rows from the front on the aisle. I place my handbag on the floor in front of my feet and cross my arms in front of me. I stare at the podium, and then away from it, above it. There's a poster. There are actually posters all over Borders, but I never notice them because usually I'm too busy looking at the books. I wonder if anyone ever notices the posters. This poster, though it's across the store from the children's books section, is a reproduction of several stamps that have been made out of beloved children's books characters. Babar. Curious George. The Very Hungry Caterpillar. Fox in Socks. One of the wild things from *Where the Wild Things Are*. The monetary value on the giant reproduced stamps is thirty-nine cents, so they're no longer current. I think I would have bought them, would have used them, had I known about them when they were issued. I stare up into the images, these images that have stood strong against the test of time and I wonder if there will ever be a Carlie stamp, if it will ever be her face gazing out from a stamp beneficently, or perhaps more appropriately, a full-body shot: Carlie mid-run. I wonder if there was, if that would be enough or if I would still think, no, it's not that, I want something else.

Outside on the street, as I hail a taxi, I assure myself that I don't think of Carlie as my child even though I must admit that I am in fact a stage mom. As I look at all the lights, the reflections everywhere, I forget for a moment where it is that I live. In the next instant I wonder why I didn't simply walk over to Eighth Avenue and get a cab going uptown. I wonder why I didn't say anything to the driver as we began our downtownward dash down Broadway, and then I remember, and I see that the taxi I'm now in is in fact going in the right direction.

I wonder if it's true. If maybe the truth is that I don't actually want children. Or at least that I don't want them as much as I want other things. Or if maybe such a thought is a form of sour grapes, seeing as I am getting on in years. I wonder if what is actually happening is that I am having my own sad little "No, really, I broke up with you first" discourse with my fertility. But if that's not it, if it turns out that I really don't want children, then what was that whole time, the irretrievable period in my life heretofore referred to as The Baby Debates, about? Other than, of course, that it led me to the acquisition of Carlie, which would make her my surrogate child, a game of connect the dots I very much don't want to complete, definitely not so soon after the evening I've just had, the company I've just kept.

I used to think I remembered the time I call The Baby Debates so well, but now as I try to recapture it, I can't. The only thing I can remember now is that maybe, throughout it, I wasn't altogether sure I wanted to win.

The taxi hits a bump and I feel overwhelmingly dizzy. I close my eyes in the hope that not seeing all the lights passing me by at such high speeds might somehow restore my equilibrium. I think of Jonathan and the years we spent on this topic that will now, for us at least, forever be closed. I think of all the discussing, all the debating, all the crying. I think of the dividing, the leaving, all done in the name of a baby, an inconceivable baby, a baby unconceived.

I didn't leave my husband because he wanted a West Highland White Terrier much more than he wanted a baby.

I open my eyes, and I let in all the passing lights and honking horns, I let in all the noises of the city, and I come so close to saying it out loud, but I don't. Whether or not I want children, whether or not I will ever have them, I didn't leave my husband because he didn't want to have children. I left my husband because he didn't love me anymore. I left my husband because I didn't love him anymore, and maybe never did.

I key into the front door of my building, walk through the vestibule and up the three flights of stairs. Carlie's been sleeping, I can tell; she comes to the door woozy, her hair looking a bit smushed, the level of hysteria thankfully low.

"Hi, Carlie," I say softly, in the ongoing hope that leaving her alone will one day be no big deal to her. She looks up at me with her liquidy and warm black eyes and answers me in kind with a flipping back of her ears and a low-tail wag.

Later, once we've gone down the stairs together, and outside quickly, and back up the stairs, once I've changed out of whatever I had thought of at the beginning of the evening as a dress that worked well for either a date or not-a-date, Carlie and I sit together on my ugly modern couch, the one I was so sure would never make me think of Jonathan, and thus hardly serves its purpose. I pull Carlie up onto my lap and I stare down into her calm eyes. She looks up at me. I wonder if she's happy,

I wonder if she's lonely. I wonder if she needs more in her life, if maybe the best thing I could do would be to get her a friend.

"Are you happy?" I ask her. She stares back at me steadily and I wonder if that is her way of saying yes, or if it's her way of saying no.

"Are you lonesome?" I ask her next. "Do you get lonesome?" I scratch the place she likes behind her ears, first on one side, and then the other. She tilts her head accordingly.

"Do you want a friend? Do you want someone? Maybe a kitty? Because I could get you a kitty," I tell her. "Do you want a kitty? If you do, if you want a kitty, you know I would get one for you."

Carlie looks up at me, and I look at her. And it's late, so I pick her up off the couch with me, and together we head into my room.

17

(carlie)

Don't Leave Me This Way!

It is not so much a kitty that I want. I would like a hen-house. And also, I would like if Amy never went to the other side of the door without me. But still, she does. For example, right now, I am alone. And still, no henhouse.

I am not positive, but I think Amy has been gone for a very long time. I think she has gone to the gym. I do not understand the gym. I do not understand why Amy does not simply run around at the dog run with everyone else, if exercise is what she has in mind. I am aware that sometimes Amy must go to the other side of the door without me; I am aware that sometimes she must leave, on occasion, for the dinner hour. I have made my peace with that as best I could. But when she leaves in her gym outfit (I recognize it instantly), though I have tried my best to envision it as a dog run for people, I find myself unable to abide the exclusion. And sometimes, when it is very dark, I have to wonder if when she goes there, to the gym, if she is one with the joggers. I have my suspicions. Because of this, when she comes back, I will not make a fuss. I will not become overly excited. I will look at her sternly, in a way that will say to her, "You did a bad thing."

Oh, no. Oh, wait. What's that? Wait just one second, it is the door! She comes back from the other side of the door! She comes back to me! I run! I run-run! I greet her at the door! I jump on her, paw on her, push on her! In case she does not know, I tell her, "You left me! You left me! You left me! You left me!" In case she has any ill-thought-out plans for a repeat performance, I shake my head, back and forth, back and forth, from the side, to the side, to the side, and then back to the side. "Don't ever leave me! Don't ever leave me! Don't ever leave me!" Then, because it is a truth, I tell her, "I love you! I love you! I love you! I love you!" and I do not mind that I have forgotten my earlier-made plans of stern rebuke. I even break out my dance moves: the one Amy calls Renfield, and from there I move seamlessly onto my side with my legs stretched out in front of me, scissor kicking in the air, mouth open in a move I have heard referred to as Wild Thing.

After my belly has been long and sufficiently rubbed, after I have done a speedy victory loop through the apartment, Amy walks to the canister in the kitchen, and one of my biscuits is removed. There are things I want more than a biscuit right now. I would like an assurance that never again will I be left alone with only the Dixie Chicks for company. I would like a salt cracker. I would like a henhouse, and yes, I would even take the kitty, just as I will right now take the biscuit. Amy smooths down the fur on the top of my head; it is long now and plumelike, and it feels nice. Amy puts one of each of her hands on the side of my face and plants a nice big kiss on my snout. All is right with the world. I am sure it always was. I follow Amy back into the kitchen. One can never tell, there could be a salt cracker. And was I, just now, in the middle of something? Was there something before that I felt it was important to say? To tell you the truth, I have no idea.

And we are on our way. We are walking, not in the direction of the First Run but rather we are walking in the opposite direction, to the place called Astor Place, and I think we are going to the subway there. And, wait just one second. It has occurred to me that the subway also means the bag. On occasion it has also meant to me cream cheese, though I am aware that the cream cheese is a bribe, even when Amy calls it Crème. I am aware also, that in its way, and this does confuse me, the cream cheese also means the bag. It is complicated, I know. The bag has now appeared and I must resist it. I do my very best Wild Thing, right there on the sidewalk. Then to my

great dismay, I am in the bag. It has been a hard morning!
I have had a hard time! If you will excuse me, I feel I need
a moment to myself.

* * *

It is now later, and I have regrouped. Amy and I have
emerged from the subway and I have heard Amy on the
cell phone, leaving a message for Renee, telling her that
if she really wants to make things up to her, then perhaps
she could arrange for a car service to take us to and fro
the set. Amy did not use the word *fro*, but I did. Amy and
I are now back at the place where they film the show, my
show, and I am sitting on the couch with an animal communicator. The animal communicator seems to think I
will have an interest in the several pieces of kibble she
has removed from her pocket. I do not have much interest in her kibble, but the fact that I have heard that she is
a communicator appeals to me. It interests me because
I have never thought people to be very good at commu-
nicating. So I decide to give her, perhaps only momentarily, my attention.

"Would you like a piece of kibble?" the animal communicator asks me, leaning down too close to me, and shaking her head, back and forth quickly from the side, to the
other side, as I myself am on occasion keen to do. I move
back, about half a space away from her on the couch, and
I look up at her with my most intent expression.

"Cream cheese," I say. And she does not hear me.

"Do you want the kibbles?" she asks me again, and I do not know why I heard, so very recently, that she was called a communicator. I do not know why she is able to call herself one.

"I want cream cheese," I say again. I stare.

"Kibbles!" she says. I stare at her intently. I make a quick jerking motion with my head toward Amy, who still holds my bag, which I believe has something to do with cream cheese, only it didn't today.

"Crème cheese!" I say. She doesn't hear me.

"Carlie, what's the problem?" the communicator asks me, in a way that I feel belies a bit of impatience.

"Crème cheese!" I say, and I feel that now I have a new understanding of the term *howling into the wilderness*.

"Do you not like your kibbles?" she asks me, and I try to tell her that first off, *kibble*, every time I have heard it, it is pronounced just like that, *kibble*. I try to tell her that adding on the *s* is superfluous and does not make me want to eat it. And also I try to tell her, *cream cheese*.

Then, Bonnie with the high voice comes in. I like Bonnie with the high voice.

"Hey, Carlie," she says to me, before prancing over to Amy to say hello to her.

"How's it going?" Bonnie asks Amy, and I hear Amy say softly that she does not think I am getting on with the animal communicator. It is a truth.

"Carlie," Amy says, walking over to me. "Is everything okay?" She pets me, and I look up into her eyes and tell her that I would like cream cheese and that while we are on the subject, could I also have a pork and manchego cheese quesadilla. Nothing.

Erin comes in, and Barton comes in. Barton suggests we take a break. He says, "Why don't you take the talent outside for a bit," and Erin asks questions and doesn't wait for answers, as I have learned is her way.

Before I hop off my couch, I take one last look at the animal communicator. I look up at her, fix her in the most defiant stare I can manage. I am all business. I am all black coal eyes. I am all rebuke, and I say to her, "Crème!"

As we leave, I hear Bonnie talking to Erin, saying she would like to wear a sparkly muumuu. And then I see that she is waving her arms over her head and singing.

"What is she doing?" Barton asks no one in particular.

"She's singing lines from 'The Age of Aquarius,'" Amy answers, and together we head to the elevator. We go down, and we walk outside to the front of the building, and around to the side of it. After we walk for a while, Amy goes over to the wall and sits down with her back against it, lightly holding on to my leash. We sit together and I feel a warm breeze blowing through the hair on the top of my head. Did I tell you that it is long now and plumelike and it feels nice?

Later, after a while, there is a shadow over us. I look up and I see a person. I am not inclined to bark at him, because I know him now. After I barked at him that first time, I sensed that though he is of a larger variety than I have become accustomed to, he is also kind.

"Hi, Nick," Amy says, and I say, "Hi, Nick," too, in greeting and in welcome, but I do not think anybody hears me. I listen to Nick say, "Can I join you," and sit down next to Amy; I busy myself with climbing over Amy so I can sit in between them. I do this because I realize that I like him, because as I told you, he is kind.

"Hi, Carlie," he says, and I climb up to him, up and onto his chest because I am interested in him. I feel he is my long-lost friend, and so I present him with my finest low-tail wag, and I see if he would like me to lick his mouth. He moves his chin from me in a way that does not offend me, but also suggests that he would not.

"How have you been?" he asks Amy, once I have settled back down.

"I've been pretty good," she says, smiling over at him. Her voice is nicer when she speaks to him than when she speaks to other people. "How have you been?"

"Good, pretty good," he says. I can feel an electricity sparking between them, and I wonder if they can feel it, too. I also feel that he wants to ask Amy something and I feel she wants to ask him something but I know that neither of them are the kinds of people who are good at asking things. Some kinds of people are, but Amy and my simultaneously new and long-lost friend here are not among them.

"I haven't seen you," he says, and then adds on, quicker, "or anyone on your set recently." Amy is not looking at him. She is looking down at her lap. But I can see that this thing he just said has made her smile. It is a quick smile and once it is gone she looks back up at him.

"We've been on location," she tells him. I know this. I was there, too.

The door opens, and Erin is there, and I feel Amy stiffen as she shields her eyes and looks up.

"Hey, you guys?" Erin says, and I see that her gaze lingers longer on Nick than it does on Amy.

"Hey," Amy says, and Nick raises his hand up, and places it back down.

"Okay, so, this is exciting? Here's a copy of the first episode? I think you're going to love it?" she says grandly, handing over a flat square to Amy. "It's brilliant?"

"Oh, wow, thanks," Amy says, "this is exciting." And I think she really does think so. And I have to say, I think so, too.

"Let me know when you watch it? I'd love to hear what you think?" Erin says. "And we're going to need Carlie upstairs in about ten minutes, okay?"

As Erin leaves, and as Amy turns the flat square over and over in her hand, Nick leans over and touches the edge of the case. "It's a big deal, the first time you see your show," he says.

"You know, it really is," she agrees, and they stare out at the parking lot together. I think they stare across the parking lot, to the river beyond it. "I think I should mark this in some way," she says, and there is something in her tone that surprises me, and I look up at her intently, though not as intently as when I was trying to get everyone to give me cream cheese.

"Maybe I'll have people over to watch it," she says, and pauses, and then she smiles. "Would you like to come? I'd like it if you'd like to come watch it, too?"

"Oh, absolutely," he says, smiling brightly at her. "Thanks. I'd love to." And I think this is good. I think the time is nigh for Amy to invite people over to our home. People other than Bonnie with the high voice, because even though I like her, very much, I feel for some reason that though she is often in our home, she has not been invited.

The three of us, we all sit together on the pavement; Nick and Amy are still leaning against the building. I am in between them. And in my heart, and in all the places where my instincts are, I am content. I rest my head gently on Amy's thigh, and I look up at her. She smiles down at me, as does Nick, and it is only then that it occurs to me that my point might have been better made were my chin perhaps placed on Nick's leg. But still, I think it is okay. I think this is a good thing. I am content.

But then two joggers approach and all is lost. I abandon my heretofore so-important-seeming chin resting as clearly, so obviously, this is much more important. I stand. I raise the hair on my hackles. Amy looks away from Nick. She looks down at me.

"Carlie," she says, "it's okay." I wonder how she can say that. I wonder how she can. When obviously it is not. It is not okay at all! There are joggers!

I run!

I run-run!

I don't actually get that far because of the dread end of the leash.

"No! No! No!" I say to them with the greatest degree of power, the utmost amount of strength. I am successful. The joggers may not have heard the right words, but they have gotten the message. They do not stop to further torment us. No, instead—and I know that this is because of me, because of my strength and bravery, because I have done my job—they obediently jog away.

18

(amy)

There Must Be Some Misunderstanding

At the time, I believed I had good reasons for inviting Erin to my apartment for Carlie's first-episode party. I thought that even though she not only changed the spelling of my name but also recast me, she does seem to care very much about the show. I thought she seemed genuinely excited and proud when she handed me the DVD on which Carlie's first moments on film, her cable television debut, have been recorded for posterity, and also, I'm told, for a focus group. I thought that it might be the right thing to do in the spirit of ongoing relations on the set. And I think I thought that if I invited Erin, it might look to Nick more like the party I said it would be, instead of looking like me and Bonnie and Renee watching TV. It seemed like a good idea at the time.

Now, as I open my door to Erin, as she hands me a bottle of red wine tied up in a pink bow and says to me, "Amy? Your building is hot pink? You live in a hot-pink building? Did you know hot pink is my favorite color?" it no longer seems like such a terrific idea.

I have given up trying to determine whether Erin is asking me a question, so I simply opt for not answering her. Instead, I thank her for the wine and take it from her. As I usher her into the living room to join the others, there are three questions I must ask myself: Why, if I just wanted to spend time with Nick, didn't I just suggest dinner rather than staging an entire party? Why didn't I assume that Renee, who always brings a date of sorts even if it is seldom a date per se, would bring a date of sorts, and that in itself would up the number of festive party guests? Why had I thought that Nick of all people would care if I had a lot of friends at my party, or anywhere else for that matter?

I place Erin's be-bowed red wine on my kitchen counter, and walk to join everyone in the living room. Bonnie is standing next to the television set already talking animatedly to Erin; Renee is sitting closely, coffee klatch–like, on the couch next to her boorish client, Keith Kelmer. He has one of those names—maybe it's because he's famous, so much more well known than most writers, or maybe it's just the alliteration—that seems to always be said in its entirety, first and last names both. I suspect that Keith Kelmer is Renee's favorite client, and I think that is because he sells the most books. I try whenever possible to avoid talk of Keith Kelmer, but am often reminded of him by Renee. She likes to put him forth as an example of a writer who always manages to write through the block. I think him very overrated, and I don't think he's very nice, and I don't think he's a very good writer. But then, he has written ten bestselling novels. In my darker moments I do wonder if maybe I should be such a not-very-good writer. I fantasize briefly about the likelihood of Keith Kelmer and Erin running away together, away to a land of bad writing and cable TV. This lightens my mood.

I walk over to stand near Nick, who has positioned himself by the small tray table, upon which rests my tea sandwich brioche. Tonight, just like the day we walked through the East Village together, Nick is not in his full *I Really Liked the Eighties a Lot* mode. Today he is more *I Thought the Eighties Were Okay, They Were All Right*. There is no eyeliner. Carlie lies at his feet, her front paw stretched out and resting lightly on his shoe.

As I come to stand next to him, somewhat at a loss for words as usual, I notice that he is enjoying the tea sandwich brioche. I myself am a great fan of the tea sandwich brioche. It is exactly what it sounds like, a large brioche within which are nestled a variety of tea sandwiches. I actually traveled all the way to the Upper East Side to get it. Nick holds one of the tea sandwiches up to me in a silent but appreciative salute. I'm pleased to see that he likes it. I'd worried as I went uptown to get it that if I really am determined not to live in the past, I probably shouldn't get my tea sandwiches there. But it's so rare that I entertain or that I serve food to anyone but Carlie, that really, I just wanted it to be nice.

"So, Amy?" Renee disentangles her attentions from Keith Kelmer long enough to crane her neck around to look behind the couch at me. "What do you think? Do you think we should get started?"

It would be a bit of a leap, even for me, to think that Nick and I were about to embark on some heartfelt conversation, so I don't despair too much at the interruption and I say, "Sure everyone, let's get started."

As I head to the DVD player with the first episode of *Things to Do in the City with Your Dog* in hand, out of the corner of my eye I see Erin sidling up to the brioche and taking a tea sandwich of her very own. Once the DVD is in place, I turn off a light or two, and join Renee and the vile Keith Kelmer on the couch. I look back at Nick, and when he sees me, he comes and sits next to me, and it's nice that he's here, it really is.

I don't have very long to linger on that feeling, though, because soon I hear Erin's voice again. "The introduction? It's really brilliant? I think it's the best part?" Carlie jumps up onto the couch to sit between me and Nick, and then the music, ever so loudly, begins to play.

A disco beat, a disco song that I actually recognize—I think because it's on my *Last Days of Disco* CD—comes blasting into my living room. It's called, if I remember correctly, "The Oogum Boogum Song." If I remember correctly, there is a lot of "Oogum oogum" and "Boogum boogum." There is some casting of spells, some "Mercy, mercy on me," and a fair amount of "getting on with your bad self." Out of the corner of my eye I can see Bonnie, moving in perfect rhythm to the disco beat. I return my attention to the television screen. I don't want to miss anything, even though I now have an inkling that it's not going to be good.

There on the screen is Bonnie, in high heels, a tight white T-shirt and a pair of bright-blue short-shorts, sashaying across the upper level of the Fifty-ninth Street Bridge, the lit-up skyline of midtown Manhattan behind her. Once I'm able to drag the majority of my attention away from the horrors of the song choice, the initial thought that forms in my mind is that it doesn't make sense, and not just in the cosmic way, but in the literal way, too. The show is about Things to Do *in* the City with Your Dog. *In!* In the city, not Things to Do Whilst en Route to the Outer Boroughs. In bright-blue short-shorts, no less. Silently, I thank the gods above that Carlie is nowhere to be seen. Though as soon as that thought is out there, as soon as I'm trying to latch on to it, to find some tiny fragment of comfort in it, I'm aware that seeing as this is after all, Carlie's show, it is only a matter of time until she appears.

Bonnie, for her part, looks really pretty, if a bit trash-ier than you'd think would be necessary for the opening sequence of a dog activity show. And even though I'd never tell Carlie this, or even Renee (not Renee in a mil-lion years), I'm very happy right now that I have been recast. Chief among my reasons is that I would not have looked one-tenth as good in the bright-blue short-shorts.

And then, the inevitable. Right as the falsetto singer of "The Oogum Boogum Song" is suggesting, "Go on, get on with your bad self," Carlie appears out of thin air and saunters next to Bonnie on the bridge. The camera pans in to her. She seems somehow to be rocking to the beat. A purple boa is tied around her neck. The words *Things. To. Do.* ricochet onto the screen. They are fol-lowed quickly by the words *In. The. City.* And then *With. Your. Dog.* Where was I when this was being filmed? I have no idea. I have failed at being a stage mom.

There are some credits, names scrolling above Carlie's head, across Bonnie's thighs. I can't read them. The song ends. The screen fades mercifully, finally, to black.

I feel a hand on my knee. I look up. Renee, her eyes wide with concern, leans in to me and whispers, "Honey, I'm just going to get you a glass of wine. Do you want red or white?"

"Red," I say numbly. My head spins. I don't say thanks. I can't thank Renee right now. Keith Kelmer gets up and wordlessly follows Renee. That's good. I can't deal with Keith Kelmer on the couch next to me.

"The part with Carlie?" Erin calls out proudly from her station by the brioche, "We did that with a green screen!? Brilliant, right?" I want to get up and run the three steps to her and take her tea sandwich from her.

I turn in my seat to look at Nick. He looks up, his eyes lock onto mine, and for a minute I forget everything else.

And in the midst of everything, in the midst of everything that is wrong with the world, and more specifically with Carlie's TV show, all I can think is, *God, I wish he would kiss me.*

"I can't believe they tracked it with *disco,*" he says in disgust.

Renee arrives with my wine, hands it to me as if ministering to the sick, and she's probably not so far off, and even though I know it's probably misplaced anger, I struggle for a moment with the urge to throw it back in her face. Partially out of concern for my ugly modern couch, and partially because I really need a glass of wine, I do no such thing.

As the actual show begins to play on the screen, I drink my wine quickly, and feel very much as if I have just been run over by a truck. But I know that hasn't happened because if I had in fact been run over by a truck I wouldn't any longer have "The Oogum Boogum Song" in my head. I worry it will remain there, stuck in my head for the remainder of my days. I am sure that in death I would be spared that. Through the confused and disoriented haze I now find myself in, I see the episode that was shot at the doggie swim place. Bonnie is running across the screen in her bikini and Carlie's there, too, looking wet and slightly annoyed. It's all very surreal, because I've already seen this before as it was actually happening, though it seemed no more real then.

When it's finally over, the only positive thought I am left with is that nothing was as bad as the opening sequence. But then that's the one part that will always be the same, the part I'll have to see over and over again, every time the show airs, for the remainder, as I believe I have mentioned, of my days. Or at least for the remainder of the show's days. I wonder how long that will be.

Eventually everyone says good-bye and filters out. Keith Kelmer is the first to go.

"Good-bye, Keith Kelmer!" I say somewhat happily because it is always the right time to say good-bye to Keith Kelmer. He's followed immediately by Renee and then Erin, neither of whom I can muster much of a good-bye to, even though I am just as pleased not to have to be in the same room with them any longer. Bonnie bounces out after them, by far the happiest of the bunch. I guess that she must have liked it, though who am I to say what this most recent upswing is really about? And then it's just Nick and me. Nick is the last man standing, or at least, the last man here.

I excuse myself to put the remains of the brioche in the refrigerator. Mostly so that Carlie will stop barking at it.

19

(robert maguire)

No One Is to Blame

Well, hello. It's been a while. Or has it? Funny thing, time. It's never made much sense to me.

In any event, when Amy returns from the kitchen, Nick is sitting on the floor in front of the empty fireplace. His knees are bent in front of him and he leans back on the heels of his hands. *Dear, sweet* Carlie skitters in front of Amy and lies down next to him with her front legs out and her back legs out, as if she thinks she's covering up a hole, or as if she now believes herself to be Superdog, flying across the floor. Either are possibilities. Amy sits down next to Nick.

"Are you upset?" he asks. He doesn't turn to face her as he asks this. He stares straight ahead at the scuffed bricks of her fireplace. She thinks there is something kind about that. I don't know. Maybe there is.

"Yes," she says, nodding, "I'm upset."

"Understandable," he says.

"You know," she says, turning to him, "I just feel like I never want to go back there, to that show. Seeing that introduction, Carlie in that boa, it just makes me want to never leave the apartment again." She blurts it out, wishing the second she says it that perhaps she had not. I myself am even slightly surprised. I thought she'd actually been doing rather well with the whole concept of "world, being out in it."

"I know how you feel," he says. *I know how you feel,* I mimic. He doesn't know the half of it. Not like I do.

"You do?" she asks.

He doesn't say anything. He runs his fingers through his hair, starting at the front and then sort of raking through all the way down to the nape of his neck. He brings his hand back down then, and rests it on his knees.

"Yes," he says. "I feel that way a lot of the time, too."

She looks right at him and her heart fills up. For a terrible moment, I fear that I will once again be gone, that Amy will forget all about me and how perfect I am for her. I squeeze my eyes shut! I clench my fists and stand firm as if I am preparing bravely to meet the apocalypse. The end of the world! Volcanoes! Floods! Fires! Brimstones! Actually, I don't know why I do this. When I do go, when Amy forces herself not to think of me, or worse yet, when she forgets all about me, it's not as if anything actually happens. It is not as if I experience any pain or duress. I simply know that I'm going, and then I'm gone. Though, really, how can you blame a fictional character for being a bit drawn to the drama of it all? It is in fact my prerogative to be dramatic. But I'm still here. I must try to focus. I must turn all of my attention back to the matter at hand.

Right as Amy is beginning to revel in the fact that what she has recognized in Nick all along is the reflection of someone just like her in his eyes, he begins to speak.

"There's actually quite a long tradition of that feeling of wanting to hide in eighties music." Amy feels disappointed at this. It is not what she hoped would happen next. In her mind, along with me, she imagines she hears a needle being scratched across a record. I tell her that in light of all the incessant references to eighties music, it is appropriate.

"Men at Work?" he continues. "'Who Can It Be Knocking at My Door?'"

"Right," she says. She feels annoyed. *Thank God.* She wants him, not song lyrics. She wants sympathy, not overintellectualism of music. She's sure there are things he has to say and that he could say them better than words written by rock stars twenty years ago. She's sure of it. Almost sure of it.

"Or what about," he says next, "'Here in my car, I feel safest of all, I can lock all my doors'?" He pauses for a moment. He looks at her and blinks. He waits. She thinks that Nick has lived so many of these moments before, that he's the type to wait, to wait for someone else to get the point. He's waiting to see if someone else will jump in and say the name of the band. She doesn't know what he's talking about, so she can't deliver his punch line. She needs someone who knows exactly what to say, and when to say it. I've tried to point this out to her before.

I wait. They don't say anything and they don't look at each other and the only thing they can hear is the low-grade electric buzz, from the cable being on but the television being off, and there is a part of Amy that feels almost unbearably sad. She thinks that if they were different, if they were more normal, then right now would be one of those moments, one of those early moments. If they were more normal, she thinks maybe she'd put her head on his shoulder, and maybe he'd kiss her. But instead they sit here, staring straight ahead, and he waits for her to remember the title of a song. I breathe in.

I try my best to point out to Amy that she has every right, every right in the world, to feel annoyed, disappointed, let down. I try my best to point out to her that she may not actually *want* him to kiss her, that what's happening here is not some big-screen romantic movie moment, what's actually happening here is that she's telling him she's upset about her dog's television show, and he's going on and on about some long-forgotten chanteur who'd like to live in his car. I exhale.

"'Cars'?" Nick says next. "By Gary Numan," he adds, and Amy just looks at him. She has no idea what to say. She believes she has lost her way in the journey.

"'Here in my car I feel safest of all.' It's from the Gary Numan song 'Cars,' off the album *The Pleasure Principle*."

She doesn't say anything. She turns away and stares at nothing in the fireplace. And if questioned later, I'd deny it, but I try to "help." I try to help her to see he's not for her at all. I try to make her see that what she wants is The Perfect Man. What she wants is me. I try to make her see that she's never going to be able to move forward with a man so mired in the past. And for good measure, I mention the fact that if she thinks about it, the two of them, they're both far too similar, they both lean a bit too much toward the reclusive. I try to point out that if the two of them ended up together they might very well never leave the house again. Hell, I even try to point that out to him, too. Desperate times, my friends. They call for desperate measures.

"You know," Nick says, after a while, "I was wrong."

She turns her head to face him. I hold my breath.

"What were you wrong about?" she asks.

"'Cars'?" he says.

"Yes?" she says.

"The song? Technically it's not even from the eighties. The album it's on, *The Pleasure Principle*, came out in nineteen seventy-nine."

He sighs, disappointed.

She sighs, too, in exactly the same way. She follows Nick's gaze back to the emptiness of the fireplace. I have achieved my goal. She thinks she needs something else, something different. She thinks that maybe what her story needs is a hero, and that she should try to find that. She tells herself it's not that she wants to be rescued. Only, maybe after more than a decade in New York City she does need to be a little bit rescued. She wonders if spending any more time on Nick would be, if you'll excuse the pun, barking up the wrong tree. She wants the hero, the leading man, the deliverer of punch lines. She wants me.

She pushes back on the heels of her hands and pushes off the ground. She turns in the direction of her kitchen, and even though it's not very far at all, she walks away.

After a few minutes, he appears, as he does have a way of doing, in the doorway of the kitchen. He knows that there had been, between them, the beginnings of a moment. He knows it is now gone.

"Well," he says. "I guess I should go." *Yes,* I think, *you should go.*

As Amy looks at him, there is a part of her that fights

me. There is a part of her that thinks, *Forget about heroes, forget about Robert Maguire, forget about being confused and about being afraid of real people because they have hurt you before.* There is a part of her that thinks, *Tell Nick not to go.* There is a part of her that thinks, *Tell Nick to stay.*

I grit my teeth and close my eyes. I wait for those thoughts to pass. I've done too much already. I can do nothing more. I can do nothing else.

"Okay," she says. "I think maybe you should go." I open my eyes. I unclench my teeth.

Quickly, they say good night. He walks back into the living room to bid farewell to *dear, sweet* Carlie. I worry this effort might gain him immeasurable points. But somehow, luckily for me, it doesn't seem to.

Nick goes.

I stay.

20

(amy)

I Need a Hero

It was one of those mornings. One of those mornings when shortly after waking up, I thought to myself, it's going to be one of those days. The fact that I'm now back at the studio and gathered in the circle of director's chairs has done nothing to make me think differently. I notice that Bonnie is, as ever, holding her stack of index cards. But the cards themselves have changed. They're now light-blue index cards instead of white ones. I wonder what it means. I think it would be good if someone in the circle, someone in a position of authority, and that would mean someone other than me, and I imagine someone other than Bonnie of the now light-blue index cards, would say something.

Soon enough, Erin gives one of those quick little *clap-claps* of her hands and says, "Okay, let's meet?"

I raise my hand. Erin looks over at me and smiles brightly. "Amy? Yes?"

I don't know why I raised my hand. I lower my hand. "I'd like to talk about the opening sequence of the show?" I begin. "For starters, I'm wondering how committed you are to 'The Oogum Boogum Song'?"

"Why's that?" she asks, still smiling super brightly.

"I don't like it," I reply.

"First?" Erin answers. "Let's start on a really positive note?" She nods at me in an encouraging and all-around joyful manner, and I think that to say it like that, all "let's *start* on a positive," doesn't really go a tremendous way in terms of accomplishing anything positive at all.

"This is really exciting?" Erin continues. She simultaneously holds up an issue of *Us* magazine and passes a stack of color photocopies to Barton, who takes one and passes the stack along. "Carlie is in *Us Weekly* this week? In the 'Stars: They're Just Like Us!' section?" she explains/exclaims. Two color photocopies are handed to me. I take one but I do not continue passing them to my right, because Carlie is to my right. I look down at my photocopy, and lo and behold, right under a picture of Rachel McAdams at the Whole Foods in Santa Monica, is a picture of Carlie. Her front right leg is outstretched. Her hair is breezing back. She is gamely crossing Second Avenue at Sixth Street. Behind her, at the other end of her red leash, is me, cut off at the knee. In addition to the lower half of my right leg, also visible are two of my fingers curving around the uppermost part of Carlie's leash. Underneath the picture is the caption: *Carlie, star of DTV's upcoming* Things to Do in the City with Your Dog, *taking a stroll in New York City's East Village*. Written across the picture in white bubbly writing is the excited sentence: "They cross the street!"

I put the photocopy down in my lap. I flip it over to its plain, white reverse side. It's better that way.

"That's really fantastic," Barton says.

"Okay, so on to the second part?" Erin continues looking right at me, and though it could just be that I have come to associate the circle of director's chairs with doom, her words suddenly sound very ominous to me. "We've shown the first episode to a focus group? And the response wasn't *exactly* what we were hoping for?" *Not surprisingly,* I think. "Now, it's not that the show isn't a success, it's more that we want it to be more of a success?" Erin explains.

Erin continues to look right at me, as if I have had anything to do with the show. I can't shake the feeling that she's somehow implying that I am to blame. I blame Erin. I look around the circle: I blame Barton. *Not what we were hoping for,* I think, and I want to shield Carlie's eyes, her ears, I don't want her to hear this. I wonder if I have, at last, lost my mind.

"So," Barton says, moving in, and now looking right at me, too. "We think it would be a good idea to brainstorm."

Out of the corner of my eye, I can see Erin's eyes light up at the very mention of the word *brainstorm*. I can almost see an exclamation point, along with a question mark of course, popping up over her head.

"I think we might want to talk about a new title for the show? Something snappy? Something a bit more descriptive of the show, something..." Erin trails off, and then she starts snapping her fingers. "*Dog and the City!*" she proudly exclaims, lifting her clipboard in the air for emphasis. And it takes so little, I think, so very, very little for me to be reminded how very much I have come to dislike her. I have a nemesis. I wonder if I always have, if there has always been someone filling this position, and I just never noticed it before.

Barton looks up languidly. He does not raise a clipboard, or any other thought-punctuating office supply, skyward. "Erin?" he says. The bright green troll-doll hair of Erin's pen dances wildly as she finishes scribbling a note across her clipboard before looking up to meet Barton's gaze.

"Yes, Barton?" she says.

"I think there's something about *Dog and the City* that refers a bit too much to another television show, if you catch my drift?"

"Well?" says Erin, "I hear what you're saying about *Dog and the City*, because you knew I was channeling *Sex and the City*, right?" Her eyebrows are raised eagerly, as if the fact that Barton has made the obvious connection means they are suddenly surfing together happily on the very same wavelength.

"Right," Barton says, "but . . ."

"Well, I think that's exactly it? I think that's part of the ironic fun?!" she says enthusiastically. A clipboard heads skyward ever so briefly before its downward descent.

Barton turns completely and faces Erin. "Bear with me," he says slowly, "I'm aware that *that* is part of the ironic fun. But I'm sure you realize that ironic fun is a dangerous game to play."

Erin, quite uncharacteristically really, narrows her eyes at Barton. Her two front teeth appear and bite down on her lower lip. I watch as her fingers curl around her now-motionless clipboard. She doesn't say anything else, and it's all I can do to look over at Barton, in awe. It's all I can do to keep myself from saying, out loud and quite loudly, *My hero.* Please note that I do not in any way mean my romantic hero. I refer to him only as a cable television show hero.

And then Carlie makes a noise. It's not a bark, it's not a growl, it's one of the conversational sounds she makes, the ones that range in tone from salutary, to impatient, to a few different levels of annoyed. I can't tell which one this is.

"All right, then?" Erin says. Her tone I can identify: it's final. "I think you all make good points?" I wonder if by "all" she is including Carlie. I wonder, did anyone pause to consider what Carlie's thoughts were? And then I have to think, *Dear God, what is happening to me?*

"Let's put this on a back burner for the time being, for right now? We can revisit it later? Let's," she says briskly, preoccupied with a shuffle of her stack of papers, a reclipping of them to her clipboard, "move on to the next?"

As soon as her papers are secure, Erin looks back up, once again bright-eyed. This won't be good.

"Also?" Erin says, looking right at me, "We've been thinking about bringing in more dogs?"

More dogs? More dogs! I hold on to my chair. I look a bit frantically toward Barton as if he really is my hero. As he stares back at me blankly, uncaringly, chewing a bit laboriously on his pen cap, I remember a millisecond too late that he is not my hero, never was. I change direction, I look down at Carlie. Carlie looks at me intently as if she's finding all the answers, figuring everything out. Or maybe that's not it, maybe that's actually just what I wish I could do.

"More dogs?" I ask. Erin grins at me. "I'm sorry, but I'm just curious, how is this the next thing on the list? I mean wouldn't this be more important than changing the title?" She doesn't seem to have an answer for that, and even though there's a part of me that is aware that the opportunity for brainstorming has now passed, I further inquire, "And then, if this is indeed happening, then why don't you just call the show *Things to Do in the City with Your* Dogs? *Dogs*, plural? Unwieldy but yet somehow accurate?" Erin scribbles something down on her pad, and I imagine it is not good.

I sit back in my chair, fuming, but yet not altogether certain why I even care. Like so many recent scenarios in my life, it's an unsettling combination. There is a part of me that cannot fathom why I care and another part of me that pipes up, a bit hysterically, to say that it's because Carlie is getting taken out of the spotlight, because it should be all about Carlie, that was the plan, for it to be all about Carlie and now it's not. Now, with everything else, it's Bonnie, it's "The Oogum Boogum Song," and now, it's *other dogs*. I don't care what I signed, this is not what I signed up for. It's not even the distant crazy cousin that no one ever mentions of what I signed up for!

I try to relax; I think I might be hyperventilating.

"Amy?" Erin says, and for a moment I worry that I have just said everything out loud.

"I thought it was supposed to be all about Carlie?" So says my inner stage mom. Only, I've known for a while now that my inner stage mom is no longer so inner. How did this happen? I think it's been far too long I've been asking myself that question about far too many subjects.

I get up off my chair, and as gracefully, and un-self-consciously as I can, I pick Carlie up and out of her director's chair and place her on the floor. I hear Erin say happily, "The other dogs would be secondary characters? They would be like backup, so Carlie would still be the primary character?"

I look up at Erin to see her head bobbing. I am about to

tell her that Carlie isn't a character, but I realize right before I say it that to do so would be hypocritical. As I start walking away, I can hear Erin saying, "A French bulldog for starters, because really, who doesn't love a French bulldog?"

"Pugs are very hot right now," Barton offers.

"Pugs are brilliant?" Erin agrees.

I look down at Carlie and she is staring up at me intently in the way she would if I were yelling or angry. I've heard it said that dogs can see colors around your body; they can actually see your aura. I don't want to think about what color my aura is right now.

"Amy?"

For a split second, I think it's Carlie who just spoke. I wish it could be. I wish she could talk and I wish I could hear her. I look up to eye level: it's Bonnie.

"Bonnie," I say, and it's only then that I notice that tears—of frustration, anger, sadness, tears at the futility of it all, I really can't say what kind they are—have welled up in my eyes. I tell myself they're not about right now. I tell myself they're cumulative. Embarrassed, I wipe quickly at my eyes.

"Hey," she says, softly, and she reaches out and puts a hand tentatively on my shoulder. "Are you okay?"

"Yes, yes," I say quickly, "I'm fine." I'm not fine. But I figure that if I am, right now, in a position where I may be able to realistically contemplate my own impending nervous breakdown, I don't think I want to burden Bonnie, of all people, with such matters. Regardless of whether she may be able to provide some insight. I look at Bonnie. She looks at me kindly. She looks at me as if she understands. I hear Barton's voice traveling out into the hall.

"Come to think of it, maybe two or three Brussels Griffons."

"Brilliant?" Erin says. "Very *As Good as It Gets*?"

"And that got an Oscar," Barton adds.

I sigh exaggeratedly.

"It's not that bad," Bonnie says to me next, and I think, *No, it really is.*

"Don't you see," I say. "Don't you see that they're ruining it? Completely? By adding so much to it? They're just taking everything and adding, and adding, and adding until anything that was good about it in the first place is gone."

Bonnie nods at me seriously. "It's what they do," she tells me.

"The TV people?" I ask.

"No," she says, "not TV people. Just people. It's what they do, and not just with TV, they do it with everything."

I look down at the floor, at Carlie. I smile down at her. Carlie can do that, I think. Even when you are least inclined to smile, even when it is the furthest thing from your mind, she can convince you otherwise. I look at Bonnie and I smile at her, too. Bonnie, in her way, has a little bit of Carlie in her. I mean that in only the very best way. It is the highest compliment I can pay.

"I just don't want to be a part of this," I begin. "I don't think I ever did, to tell you the truth. I think I've known for months that I should stop all this nonsense and just write my book." And then I keep talking. It appears I am on a roll. "And it's not even months, you know?" She nods. Maybe she does know. "It's years. Years and years, I've been walking around feeling as if I had so much homework to do, and talking about it, and staying home, since ostensibly that's where you have to be to do the homework? And I've barely done any of it? I've barely done anything of what I've set out to do."

She nods at me sympathetically. "It must be really hard to be a writer in New York," she says to me, and I think it's nice of her that she said that, that she called me a writer. She didn't need to. She was, after all, already on my good side.

"Yes," I say in agreement, "I guess it is." I smile at Bonnie, a strange appreciation for her, for her presence, washing over me.

"I think it's really hard to be anything in New York," she says next, and I have to wonder if in fact Bonnie is secretly a brilliant sage, a centuries-old wise man.

"Thanks," I say. Bonnie bends down to pet Carlie, and I look down, too. There's something nice about seeing the way Carlie swans around whenever Bonnie's near.

"Amy," Bonnie says, looking up at me seriously, very seriously.

"Yes," I say.

"Have you seen this on Carlie's nose?" I bend down, noticing as I do that Carlie is not swanning around the way she generally does in Bonnie's presence. I take Carlie's nose gently in my hands. I notice as I do that she doesn't squirm or try to get away, I notice as I do that I think Carlie's looking up at me a bit sadly. Across the black ridge of her nose is a smattering of flesh-colored spots, almost the exact color as the inside of her ears, almost pink. I rub my hand over her nose, the spots don't go away, the spots are part of her nose now.

"Oh, gosh," I say to Bonnie. "I didn't see this earlier? I don't think I saw this five minutes ago." Bonnie looks from me to Carlie with concern. I get a pain in the pit of my stomach even as I tell myself it's nothing. I wonder, *Do Carlie's eyes look glassy?* Or do they always look a little glassy? I can no longer remember, and the pain in my stomach grows. I pull Carlie to me. I stand up with her, holding her, and ask her, "Carlie, are you all right?" She looks at me in a way I would really have to say was woefully. Or is it miserably? *Oh, God.*

"Do you think it's a problem?" Bonnie asks me, standing up along with us, leaning over to pet the top of Carlie's head.

"It could be a problem," I say.

Carlie starts twisting around, squirming around to be put down. I hear a little grunt. This isn't wholly unusual; Carlie's not what anyone would call a lapdog. She's very busy, she doesn't often have time for too long a cuddle. Sometimes when I pick her up I imagine her saying, "Amy, I have five minutes, not longer." I put her down, telling myself again that everything is okay.

Just as I'm standing up, I hear an *mmblah* coming up from the floor. Carlie's breakfast lies in a puddle by my feet. I look up at Bonnie, whose eyes are now brimming over with concern. It's not as if I'm unfamiliar with dog-gie throw-up. In the past several years, I have seen my fair share. But there is a part of me, a really terribly huge part of me, that thinks this is a lot worse than I am even aware.

"I think I have to go," I say to Bonnie, urgently. "I think I have to take her to the vet."

"Yes, yes," she says back to me. "You go. I'll tell Barton and Erin, you just go."

"Okay," I say quickly, bending down to pick Carlie up, leaning in to kiss her head. "Okay," I say again, to no one in particular, not even to myself, because I do not in fact think that anything is okay. "Okay."

I hurry past the elevator. I don't feel I have time to wait for it. Together, Carlie and I head for the stairs.

21

(amy)

Heaven Knows I'm
Miserable Now

I'll hail a cab, I think as I run down the three flights
of stairs with Carlie in my arms. Do they even have
taxis driving around in Long Island City? It is among the
many things I've never taken the time to notice. Luckily,
I spot a cab lingering on the corner, the moment we step
out onto the street. Luckily, thankfully, the driver is not
one of the legions of dog-hating cab drivers, and we're on
our way in a flash.

I give the driver my own address on Fifth Street;
Carlie's vet office is right across the street from my apartment. I vaguely remember its proximity being one of the
pros on the list I'd made for myself about the building;
that and the door I liked so much on the building a few
doors down had somehow worked together to assuage

any misgivings I might have had about the hot-pink exterior of the dwelling I was about to inhabit. Twenty-five blessedly traffic-free minutes later, I all but throw two twenties at the driver as we pull up outside my hot-pink building. As I exit the cab and hurry across the street, I think none of that matters now, not in the slightest.

I hold Carlie and walk carefully down the three cement steps, through the door, the vestibule, and into the waiting room.

The receptionist, who vaguely knows me from Carlie's vaccination appointments and checkups, looks up and greets me as Mrs. Dodge. I don't know why. I've never called myself "Mrs." here. I try to remember if I called ahead, if I called at some point from the studio or at some point in the taxi to say I was on my way. I can't remember.

"Hi," I say, still holding Carlie to me, close and over my shoulder, and, I realize, like a baby. "I don't think Carlie's feeling very well. She has spots on her nose and she seems a bit out of sorts. She threw up her breakfast about half an hour ago." The nurse nods at me gravely and reaches for her phone, pressing buttons on the keypad. I know she's saying something, but I can't hear what it is. It's as if my brain is all filled up at present. It's as if I simply don't have the psychic space left to comprehend any more language. I feel Carlie's little body spasm, followed by the feeling of dog vomit trailing down my back.

"Oh, goodness," says the receptionist. One of the vet

techs arrives to tell me that he's going to take Carlie to an examination room. He leans in and takes her from me.

"I'm coming, too," I say to the vet tech. He looks at me like he wishes I wouldn't, but he doesn't try to stop me. I follow right behind them, reaching out to hold onto Carlie's paw.

Carlie and I are only in the small examination room for a minute when a vet walks in. It's a vet I've never met before.

"Mrs. Dodge?" he says walking in, consulting a chart in his hand.

"Ms. Dodge," I correct. "Or Amy. Amy," I repeat, settling on that.

He reaches out with his hand. "I'm Dr. August Tarquin, it's very nice to meet you." I shake his offered hand but I do so with protest in my heart. I don't want a new vet. I want an old one.

"She threw up," I tell him by way of greeting. "Twice. And she has pinkish spots on her nose."

He smiles at me with assurance. I can see how his confident manner and his relaxed calm could be assuring to other people. It's not to me. He leans down to Carlie and shines a mini flashlight in her eyes. He holds on to her nose to get a better look. She sits patiently and lets him. Then the new vet walks the few steps to the exam room door and opens it slightly. In the next instant the vet tech is back.

"Ken," Dr. Tarquin says to me, "is just going to take Carlie to the back." I stare blankly back at him for a moment. Before I can fully consider if I should do anything to stop it, renegotiate the contract terms or something, Carlie has been hoisted off the exam table and carried to the door.

I look up at her retreating face and I think she looks concerned, and oh dear God, I have to say I think she looks a little frightened. Generally, especially in light of recent events, recent revelations, recent dates with editors from Argonaut Press, and recent adventures in cable television, I try to refer to myself, in relation to Carlie, only ever as Amy. But at this moment as she's leaving the room far too quickly, everything feels far too much out of my control. All bets? They're off.

"Mommy's right here!" I call out after her, and as I look back over at the vet, it's true, I do wish that I'd gone with "Amy." But how can I even think of that at a time like this? I tuck an unruly and frazzled piece of hair behind my ear.

"Well, then," the vet says to me next. I feel like I might be only moments away from receiving news that will change my world. The ground is about to fall out from under me. I stare back at the vet blankly, like a guppy. I am floating purposelessly, aimlessly, trapped inside a glass bowl.

"We're just going to draw some blood, and take a look

around," he says, and horrible images fill my mind. He pauses for a moment, and I wonder if he's waiting for me to speak. He could be. He could have no way of knowing that I can't speak, that I'm frozen, that were I to somehow speak it would only be to tell him that I am so close to really freaking out. And maybe it has to do with more than Carlie, maybe it does. I am willing to concede that point.

"We're going to take an x-ray, make sure there isn't any sort of obstruction that could be causing the vomiting," he says softly. "I don't think there is," he adds, "but just to be safe." The thought of Carlie, laid down quietly on an x-ray table, the thought that maybe some obstruction will be found, one that is the result of my leaving something lying around that I should have thought to put away, brings tears to my eyes. I wonder, as I nod at him, whether it's possible to conceal them.

He nods back at me, and I don't think it is. For the second time today I am self-consciously wiping away tears. And now, also, I'm trying not to think of Carlie confronted not by the vastness of her fame, but rather by an x-ray machine.

"I'm just going to look up a few things with regard to the disco on her nose," he tells me next.

"The disco on her nose?" I ask.

"Oh, sorry," he says, smiling. "Discoloration. In vet school, you use so many abbreviations to study, they have a way of taking over."

"Right," I say. Vet school? Was he just in vet school? Should he maybe not bring something like that up, right now, right in front of the worried and slightly ill-at-ease patient's person? I look at the vet standing in front of me and notice for the first time that he's handsome (ish), blond hair, square jaw, a little bit of a tan. But that's not important. What is important is that he looks to be in his mid- to late thirties. So unless this is a second career for him, which in itself would be cause for some concern, hopefully he's not fresh out of veterinarian school. I decide it would be best if I could refrain from inquiring.

"Okay, so you hang tight," he says. He motions to a chair in the corner of the room, and then he places his hand down on the examination table. He pats the table twice, quickly, in an "all set" type of way. There is, in his manner, a nonchalance; a nonchalance that seems to say, *This is nothing, this will all be fine, Amy, everything will be okay.* I'd like to find a way to hold on to that implication. In lieu of physically holding on to an implication, I am for a moment overwhelmed by the urge to hold on to the vet.

"I'll be back in shortly," he says, "and we'll talk."

"Okay," I say and try to get hold of myself, to somehow find my center. "Okay," I repeat. I sit down in the chair, and settle in to stare at the wall. I feel it's a good thing that no one has suggested that I venture back to the waiting room. I feel that right now I really need to be where other people are not.

"Okay," he says and looks at me kindly. His eyes are liq-uidy, not as if there are tears about to spring out of them, but liquidy the way Carlie's eyes are, in the way that I think conveys calm, a kind of calm unattainable to me. I think for a moment that Dr. Tarquin is going to reach out and place his hand over mine, but he doesn't. He turns and opens the door, then closes it softly behind him.

I take a deep breath, and I look around the small room. I notice that almost everything—surfaces, walls, various accoutrements—is either light blue or chrome. I lean back in my chair. I close my eyes.

And when I hear a soft rap on the door, as if it's me and not Carlie who has come to the doctor's office, as if there is the need to be sure I'm dressed, or undressed rather, but properly wrapped in my robe, I wonder if there is a nonchalance in that knock, if in it I could find the implication that everything will be okay.

"Yes, come in," I say. I have no idea how long I've been in here waiting; my watch has been broken for forever. Dr. Tarquin enters and clears his throat. If I were actu-ally having an out-of-body experience—as opposed to traveling through the last few years of my life with the constant unsettling sensation that I was in the middle of one—I imagine I would see myself here, in the corner of this small room of chrome and light blue, staring point-lessly into space. I look up at the vet. I attempt a smile. I'm almost certain the smile falls very short of success.

He smiles back at me; his smile isn't nearly as faulty. "Amy," he says.

"Yes," I say, and I don't, or I won't, or I can't breathe out. Dr. Tarquin breathes in, and I know, I know his next sentence is not going to be about how everything is fine.

"We're going to need to keep Carlie here overnight," he says, and pauses, and my eyes fill with tears.

"It's okay," he says softly, but with less of his earlier nonchalance. "Our main concern is that she's quite dehydrated." Dehydrated? Dehydrated is something you can blame a person for. It's something that can be avoided. If only, I think, more time had been spent by me drawing Carlie's attention to her water dish, getting down on all fours and splashing around in it.

"Because of the vomiting," he adds, and I look back up at him. I am, just for the smallest second, relieved. I nod again. I'm sure it's the only thing I can do.

"And we want to keep her on IV fluids." I nod.

"And we'd like to monitor her, of course." I nod.

"And we'll run some tests, and we'll try to get to the bottom of the discoloration, make sure it's nothing to worry about." I nod.

"Uh-huh," I start to say. "Uh-huh, uh-huh," I repeat again. Each word he speaks seems to fall down on me like bricks falling off an only partially built but somehow already doomed building. "Uh-huh."

"We'll get to the bottom of this," he says reassuringly,

reaching a hand out, placing it once again on the examination table between us. I look at his hand, outstretched there between us. I look at the way the cuff of his white coat has ridden up, revealing the French cuff of his shirt sleeve, the white cotton folded back and held in place by a cuff link in the shape not of a dog as one might expect, but inexplicably of a submarine. I look up at him, and I meet his eyes.

"We?" I ask.

"I'm sorry?" he says, the skin around the corners of his eyes crinkling.

"Who is we, I mean? Who else will be with Carlie?" I ask.

"Well, we've—all of us here at the hospital, we've got an excellent team of VTs—that's vet techs—and someone will be here around the clock with Carlie, she'll be receiving really excellent care. I myself will be here until nine."

I am able to see how that all makes sense, how it could even be reassuring. Only it isn't to me.

"Does she have to stay over? I mean, is that an absolute? Because, really I'd be fine if you'd like to give me an IV? I can set her up?" I suggest. "Or, perhaps even someone, one of the VTs, the, uh, the vet techs could come to my apartment and set her up with her IV there?" Between all the initials, as I wade through a seemingly endless loop of V and T and I and V, I am aware on some level that I have just suggested, as if it were the most normal thing in the world, that the staff of the veterinarian's office decamp to my apartment and set up shop there. It may already have been too long that my dog has been a future veritable star of the small screen.

"Or," I begin again, anew, "I could just make sure she drinks her water. Sometimes, if I put an ice cube in her water dish, she finds it very interesting, and then just the investigating of the ice cube, she'll get a good amount of water in that way." I can feel my head nodding vigorously up and down, up and down. I can almost perfectly envision the guppylike bulging of my eyes.

Dr. Tarquin doesn't look convinced, not nearly, but he is listening. I think it's possible that he could be considering my suggestions, so, really, I have no choice but to continue.

"Or I could get her Gatorade!" I say, and suddenly, I find it impossible to stop. "She really likes Gatorade, mostly just the red Gatorade, but that shouldn't be a problem, right? It's not as if it's terribly hard to find red Gatorade. That's one of the things people say is so great about New York, right? That you can get whatever you want, whenever you want at any time of day or night, and you can even get it delivered?"

I watch as his hand reaches out again, but this time he doesn't rest it on the examination table between us, instead he reaches out a bit further and he puts his hand on my arm; he's trying to stop me in my crazed attempt to pick up every last one of the bricks that fell down on me earlier, from the partially constructed and crumbling building that is my life. But I don't want to be stopped, and I'm running out of time.

"And of course I'll stay up with her myself all night. I mean I can drink some of the Gatorade, too, and I'll keep a close watch on her nose, on the pigmentation. I can write it down, I can keep a journal, and we'll come right back in the morning. We live right across the street."

I reach out with my free arm, putting my hand out and onto his arm. We stand there for a moment like two wrestlers holding on to each other in some sort of bizarre nelson grip. Then, at exactly the same moment we both remove our hands. As we both return our hands to our sides, I start to look away, but something in his expression holds my eyes.

"Amy," he says. "I understand how you feel, believe me I do, but it's really the best thing for her to stay here, to stay hydrated, to stay on fluids, to stay under observation." Stay, stay, stay. "Trust me," he adds, and I think reflexively *no* and then, *why* and then, *why you?* "She'll be under excellent care." And there's finality there, in his voice, and while I may not be very good at recognizing things, I think I do know a little bit about finality. Here it is again.

There is something, I tell myself, to knowing when

to walk away, to knowing when you're not going to win. And in the midst of all of this, I want to file that bit of knowledge away. I'm pretty sure it's a lesson I haven't completely learned, not in the way that I should have.

"Okay, I understand what you're saying," I say. The vet nods his head at me. The standoff is over, but not before I have the chance to add, "I'd just like to see her. Can I see her again please, before I go?"

"Yes, of course, certainly," he answers swiftly, as he turns away from me and moves the few small steps to the door, "just one moment."

He's gone again, and again, the way time passes is so confusing. I don't know how anyone ever even tells time. I sit back down in the chair, and I wait. I have no idea for how long.

The wait is simultaneously too long and not nearly long enough, because when Carlie returns, carried off to the side almost like a football by the vet tech, the look on her little face, in her little eyes, is such a combination of fear and bravery that I am undone. I am completely at the mercy of my own overwhelming emotions. I don't even realize I've started to cry, loud and messy un-self-conscious crying in the examination room with the vet tech right there, with the vet lingering behind us.

As I reach out to Carlie, I notice the vet tech has an intricate tattoo snaking down his arm to his wrist. The tattoo does nothing to make me feel better because if a person is going to put himself through what really must be a fair amount of pain for the sake of what, for the sake of rebellious statement, how kind is he going to be to animals, to my animal? As I take Carlie from him, briefly grazing his tattooed arm in the process, I realize it's a pointless concern. I know, perhaps better than most, that the way people treat themselves, the way people treat other people even, often has no similarity at all to the way they are to animals.

Carlie is with me now, and I hold her against me, her front paws on my shoulders right up close to either side of my neck. Her back legs are too short to reach around my waist, but that does not stop her from trying. As I feel her little legs squeezing into my stomach, in a vain attempt to hold on, it's all I can do, or maybe it's more than I can do, to remind myself that the crying at this point really needs to morph into a more dignified type of crying.

I wipe at my eyes, with one hand and then the other, trying my best not to jostle or displace Carlie, who nonetheless feels the movement, and burrows her wet and, I am reminded, strangely discolored, nose into the crook of my neck. And all other thoughts, the ones about maintaining a level of composure to the tears, are lost.

"You can bring in a T-shirt, if you'd like, and I can put it in her cage with her," the vet tech offers, and the word *cage* doesn't help.

No one says anything for a moment, not the vet tech, nor the vet, who has made his way over to the counter on the far (though still, quite near) side of the room, and is preoccupied with the lifting of various chrome canister covers and the inspection of cotton balls, and unnaturally long wooden Q-tips. I take a deep breath, and slowly, as if moving underwater, I place another kiss on Carlie's mottled nose, and I hand her over to the vet tech. He wraps his tattooed arms around Carlie, and I take another deep breath.

"T-shirt?" I inquire.

"Yes," he says. "Best that it's a T-shirt you've already worn. Without washing. You can bring it in anytime, and I'll put it with her, and she'll smell you. It helps them, it makes them feel you're there with them." I don't even bother with the wiping away of tears that haven't even yet started to fall.

"Okay, thanks," I say, and though I consider taking off the very dog-vomit-covered shirt I'm wearing, the only upper-body clothing I have on other than a bra is this shirt. I make the executive decision to leave the vet's office with my shirt, if nothing else, intact. "I'll run home right now and bring it right back," I add on.

"We'll be here," he says. In my mind, I'm already picturing my laundry basket, going to it, selecting from it the most comforting T-shirt I can find and bringing it back here hastily to Carlie. And I think that I'll bring her stuffed duck, too. She loves her stuffed duck. She carries it around with her from room to room. She likes to rest her head up on it.

"Can I bring Carlie her duck?" I ask. "Carlie has a duck," I add, perhaps a bit maniacally.

"Yes," he says, "by all means."

And then Carlie's gone, and the vet tech is gone and his tattoos are gone and it's just me and the vet who is no longer so preoccupied with his canisters of cotton balls and he has turned around to face me. I don't know when he turned around. He hands me a tissue.

"Uh, thanks," I say, hastily taking the tissue, which is not as it turns out a tissue but a handkerchief. An actual grandfatherly handkerchief. I look down at the monogram, stitched in the shape of a diamond in navy blue thread. Little A, big T, little J. I try not to think about the state of my nose, its level of redness, what might be dripping from it. "I'm so sorry," I say.

"No," he says, shaking his head, "don't be." I turn my back to him and blow my nose. I take a deep breath, and as I let it out, I nervously fold the handkerchief over itself and over itself, before reaching a hand across the examination table and handing it back to him.

"I guess you're used to this," I blurt out next. "I mean, does everyone get this upset about their dogs?" I am not sure if the question is meant to be rhetorical or not.

"No," he tells me, and I think there must be something

to be said, somewhere, for honesty. "But I wish every-one did," he adds warmly. He reaches out and touches my sleeve again. "We'll give you a call first thing in the morning."

"Right," I say, "okay, first thing tomorrow." His hand is gone from my arm, and I nod again, and say, "thanks," maybe twice, I'm not sure. I turn to go, to finally leave this room, to go home quickly to retrieve a T-shirt and Carlie's stuffed duck, and to come right back.

22

(carlie)

Promises

Do not worry. I will be fine.

23

Mirror in the Bathroom

Quickly!

Quickly, I go home. Quickly, I grab a T-shirt from the laundry, though I do take some extra time to root down to the bottom of the laundry basket. My hope is that the dirtier the T-shirt, the gamier the T-shirt, the better to provide comfort and a sense of safety to the ailing and caged (*oh God, caged*) Carlie. And also, even under the best of circumstances, Carlie is a great fan, a studied connoisseur of dirty things. I select a T-shirt and grab a pair of running shorts for good measure.

Quickly again after the momentary pause, I locate Duck and dig out a tote bag from underneath the bed. There is still some outwardly aware, socially accept-able part of me that remains, and it feels it would be questionable to run willy-nilly across the street with dirty laundry and a stuffed duck.

And then I'm there, I'm across the street again. I'm in the vet's office, and I am removing items from my tote bag, one by one, and handing them gingerly, and perhaps not as apologetically as one would think necessary, to the vet tech. I no longer have any idea what his name is, and I wonder if I ever did. He still has his tattoos. Like so many other things, the tattoos have not simply vanished just because I would prefer it that way.

"She likes to put her head on her duck," I say as if it is a matter of the utmost importance, because it is. I hear Carlie's bark coming from the back.

The vet tech puts a finger to his lips. "Shh," he says. "I think she hears you."

"Can I go back?" I whisper.

"No," he tells me, and I'm gone again, back across the street again, before I start to cry again.

When I get back up to my apartment, I don't reach for the light switch by the door. I feel my current state is not one for brightness. I want a candle; I want the flickering light. I think maybe the scent of mimosa, with its purported soothing qualities, could help. I grab a matchbook from my matchbook vase, even though the part of me that tries to remain vigilant in these matters, regardless of what else is going on, reminds me that the matchbook vase, especially at this juncture, may not be the best idea.

I think that I don't care. I think that most of all I want to light a candle.

Only after I've lit the candle do I take notice of the matchbook. The one I've pulled out of the vase is from Parioli Romanissimo, a restaurant that used to be in a townhouse on Eighty-first Street, right off Fifth Avenue, but has long since closed. It was so beautiful there, and so expensive. I turn the matchbook over in my hand and wonder how long I've had it. Close to a decade, I think.

It's as if my life up until now has been lived underneath sea level, underneath a drain in a bathtub, and someone has only just now come along and pulled the plug out of the drain above me. All the water, all the filthy, dirty, long-gone-cold water is pouring down on top of me.

I remember my brief fascination with the collecting of matchbooks, with assembling a collection that would document all the places I'd been. I spent a zealous year taking a matchbook from every place I went, every restaurant, every hotel. I thought there was something meaningful about it. It wasn't just going out to dinner; if it was going out to dinner and keeping a record of it, it somehow meant more. I kept all the matches in a beautiful, delicate Art Deco vase. The vase filled up quicker than I'd expected, because we went out to dinner so often, to drinks, and to events. We were a fancy couple, Jonathan and I, and we lived the fanciest of fancy lives. And around the time it was filled, before I'd even begun to think about designating another vase, Jonathan had, unconsulted on the matter, spoken up as if out of nowhere, as if from the underside of a great drain himself.

"You know," he said. "I was thinking, maybe let's cool it with the matchbook collection?"

"Cool it with the matchbook collection?" I had repeated, in a way that was not so much repeating, as it was incredulous asking.

"Yes," he'd said, not missing a beat. "I've never liked them, I've always thought of them to be fairly middle class, you know? Kind of common?"

For fear of appearing fairly middle class, kind of common, I hadn't argued the point. I hadn't insisted that the matchbook collection continue on, uncooled.

But I had managed to say, with what I thought was a tone almost completely void of hostility, "That's fine, but I want to keep the matches I already have, the ones already in the vase."

He'd narrowed his eyes briefly at said vase. "Is that from the gallery?" he asked.

"I don't know," I lied. And that was the end of it, and the matchbook collection was over. It did not grow and evolve to record the years we shared. The collection stayed on a shelf in the study, for the most part unchanged, only every so often, when we traveled, I'd spirit away a book of hotel matches, and upon our return home, I would bring them to the vase, and shove them down to the bottom.

I look at the glass vase, filled as it is to its brim with matches I haven't collected in years. I am struck by the impulse to light one match and drop it into the vase, to watch the explosion that would happen, to stare mesmerized at the subsequent fire. I am struck by the impulse to throw the matchbooks one by one, out the window. Coco Pazzo, Palio, Ferrier, The Lobster Club, La Goulue, Fred's, places that either no longer exist or that I haven't been to in years. I want to be able to make it so that none of them ever existed at all.

If I throw the matchbooks out the window, they'll land on the street. They'll still be out there. Even if all the matches get stepped on or thrown away, or even just kicked into the gutter, they'll still be out there. There needs to be another way. And I think I can save the vase.

I dump all the matchbooks onto the brick bottom of my nonworking fireplace. I try not to think of how it is among Carlie's favorite places to lie and while away an afternoon. I try not to think how, much in the manner of Duck, this fireplace gives her great comfort. I light a match, quickly, bravely, and just as quickly, though more resignedly than bravely, I hesitate. I blow it out. I leave the matchbooks there, scattered across the floor of the fireplace, because I know suddenly that all these matchbooks are only symbols. I could burn them or throw them out the window, I could run, glass vase in hand, to the FDR Drive and across it and dump the vase and its contents in its entirety into the East River. I could do any number of destructive things, but I see now what I have always known but am only beginning to understand. No matter what I do, no amount of fire, or water, or anything else, will make the memories go away. No matter what I do, they'll always be there. What I need to do is to stop losing sight of the fact that they're just that: memories.

I drop the blown-out match onto the floor of the fireplace. I lean back, my hands behind me, my knees bent, in a way that reminds me of sitting here with Nick, and I close my eyes.

I have no idea how long I'm there before the phone begins ringing, before its insistent, persistent shrill brings me back to the present, sitting in front of the fireplace, the scattered remnants of my memories laid out on the floor all around me.

I push myself off the floor and head to the kitchen, where the phone is waiting in its charger.

"Yes, hello?" I say.

"Miss Dodge?" I hear, and I think it's the vet. I've only ever heard his voice one time, but I'm sure that it's him.

"Yes?" I say. "This is she. Dr. Tarquin?"

"Yes," he says, and as he says it, as that one small monosyllabic, generally agreeable word travels through the phone line to me, I think that he must be calling because of Carlie, that of course he's calling because of Carlie, and my heart sinks. I have nothing to hold on to.

I sit down on the floor. I have nowhere to put my head, and I think I might need somewhere to put my head. I lean forward until my head is resting on the floor. From somewhere emptying out and almost hollow inside me, I hear myself say, "Is everything all right?" It's as if it's being said by someone else entirely.

"Oh, I'm sorry," he begins, "I didn't mean to worry you. Carlie's resting comfortably, and she's well hydrated, and we just have to wait on the one test to come back, and that'll be in the morning. I'm confident she'll be fine."

"Oh," I say, relief and happiness both washing over me. "Okay, thanks."

"Miss Dodge?" he says.

"Call me Amy," I say, and I wonder why he's called.

"You left your tote bag here," he says next, answering my unasked question.

"My tote bag?" I ask, thinking of Duck.

"Yes, I wanted you to know it was here."

"Oh," I say. I think that this is not a phone call he needed to make, that he could just as easily have left it to someone on his staff, to the vet tech with all the tattoos. I think this is a vet. This is a man who saves lives, and not just any lives, but animals' lives, dogs' lives. I think my mother would approve.

"Amy?" he says again. I think again, *This is a man who saves lives.* I will not let myself think a thought so absurd and antifeminist as, *Maybe he might save mine.*

"Oh, I'm sorry, Dr. Tarquin," I say, trying to snap back to reality.

"Call me August," he says. *Oh,* I think. I walk with the cell phone the very short distance out to the living room, and I stand in front of the fireplace. I look down at the matchbooks, at the detritus of my past. I think of the past, the present, and the future and how I can focus on any of them that I choose. I have the choice. I think that Carlie—Carlie who's fine now, so says Dr. Tarquin—is so good at living in the present, has such an easier time of it than I ever do. I think that this, right now, this phone call is a door, a door that's opening, and that I should go to the other side of it. I think that Carlie would tell me to do that, if she could. I think she'd tell me it's a good thing to see what's on the other side of the door.

"Yes," I say, "you know what, August? If you're going to be there, I'll just run right over and get my bag now?"

"Oh, take your time," he says. "I'll be here."

I'll be here, I repeat in my mind, and I think that's good and I like something about that, something about the way that sounds. As I hang up, I quickly get all the matchbooks put away. I head into the bathroom and look in the mirror. My eyes are a bit puffy at present. I wash my face and pull my hair back. I reapply a casual but still appropriately mournful bit of makeup.

In a few minutes, I'm going to head out the door to the vet's office, for the third time in this very long day.

24

(robert maguire)

Tempted

For a moment, I am hazy. I am confused as to why I am here, as surely this is not a romantic time, what with the young and crafty Carlie having fallen so gravely and drastically (and, I am quite sure, not actually) ill. Though I am also very pleased, quite overjoyed actually, to know that I do exist in other moments, moments not romantic. And, truthfully, circumstances demand things of me. It's not as if either Amy or Carlie is in any state to narrate right now. So as a gentleman, and as an adventurer of course, I feel it is nothing short of my duty to step in.

There is music playing in the background. It is one of those bands of which that Nick is so fond—the Smiths—but Amy doesn't notice it. She doesn't listen to the music, let alone to the words. She gathers her things, grabs her handbag, and even though the sky has long been dark, she grabs her sunglasses and puts them on her head before she heads out the door.

When she reaches the bottom of the stairs and steps out onto the street, she sees that vet, Dr. Tarquin, there, across the street. He's standing right outside the vet office. He holds her empty tote bag in his hand. He's been waiting for her. I do not know for how long. Amy crosses the street without bothering to walk all the way to the corner and the crosswalk, without looking both ways. I watch him standing there. I see him the way Amy sees him. And then I know exactly why I'm here. It is not, as I had hopefully suspected, because my sphere of influence is increasing. Alas. It is because when Amy looks at the vet, there is—I can see it now—romantic interest.

"Hi," she says, as she steps up onto the sidewalk and stands next to him. "Thanks," she adds, reaching out for the tote bag he holds in his hand, crumpled up like an article of discarded clothing. She takes her tote bag from him, wondering why he is in fact out here, on the street. He seems to pick up on her unasked query. *Perceptive,* I think. Though I would imagine it must be necessary to be perceptive in his line of work.

"Ken mentioned that when you came earlier Carlie heard you, so I thought it'd be better to meet you out here," he explains. *So thoughtful.* I hope this one isn't going to turn out to be a problem for me as well. I can't help thinking that I only just managed to get rid of the last one.

Amy is reminded again of *dear, sweet* Carlie in a cage. She hopes she is resting her head on Duck for comfort and she wonders if she should not have even come here, under the circumstances, even though she has reason to believe that the circumstances are okay. She wonders if she should have said, "Please, just put the tote bag with Carlie."

"Amy?" he says.

"Oh," she says, looking back up at him. "Sorry."

"Are you okay?" he asks.

"Yeah. Yes," she says. "I'm just a little spaced out. It's been a long day."

"I know," he says. She looks up at him, tilts her head at him, and wonders, *Does he really know?* She's not sure such a thing could be possible, and they stand in silence for just a few moments more, before he adds, "So, listen, like I said, she's well hydrated, and it's really just a matter of waiting for the test to come back, and most likely, it's nothing."

"Yes, right," she agrees, nodding, trying to shake off any lingering gloom.

"So, listen," he says. She notices his hand running through his wavy hair, and then being placed, fidgety, into his pocket. He's a bit fidgety, this one, if I do say so myself. "Can I buy you a drink?" he asks.

She smiles at him, and says, "Yes, I'd like that."

They walk together, just one block up, and then only a few doors down, to a quiet bar with dark wood walls and dark wooden stools. One or two brightly lit signs advertising beer adorn the walls. As they settle side by side on two bar stools, Amy tells herself that she should not think of me. Why does this keep happening? I would really so much rather stay. All this recent trying not to think of me makes me very nervous, very worried, very threatened. And I have to say, with all the work I've done lately to keep myself around, I've been starting to feel a bit exhausted. There are days I wonder how much longer I can go on. But what can I do except try to fight?

"Run, Amy, run!" I say loudly and really rather self-ishly. I am surprised actually at how selfish I have in recent weeks become. But self-preservation is a serious matter. I ask you, how can it not lead to selfishness? But still, I'm gone.

*   *   *

And I'm back. I have reason to believe it is the same evening and that I have not been gone very long at all. As it should be. Amy and the vet—I no longer wish to speak his name—have emerged from the dark bar, and together they have returned to Fifth Street. They stand together outside her door. She does not wish that he would quickly walk away.

"Can I call you?" he asks her. *Can I call you?* I mimic. Be a man, I say! If you want to call her, just call her.

"Well, of course, I mean, you're going to call me first thing in the morning to tell me about Carlie's test results, right?" Amy replies matter-of-factly.

"Well, yes, of course," he says, and then he blushes slightly.

"Fraud!" I say as loudly as I can. "Sissy!"

"But after that," Sissy Boy continues. "After everything is okay with Carlie? I was hoping I could call you about things that don't have anything to do with Carlie?" He leans in to her as he says this.

"Everything has to do with Carlie," she says. (This, I know. *Believe me*, I know.) Amy smiles at him as she says it, and I am surprised because these days it is so rare that she has any sense of humor at all. And then the vet leans in farther, and he leans down slightly, and he kisses her. I do my best to point out to her that perhaps this is not ethical. I try to explain that perhaps this knight-in-shining-armor act is just that, an act. But I no longer have her full attention.

"Well, good night, then, Amy," the vet says, smoothly.

"Good night," she says, and is that just the hint of a sparkle I see in her eye?

Then, to add insult to injury, we have to stand there and watch him as he saunters slowly back across the street.

25

(carlie)

Together, We Will Go Our Way

The doctor is here. They call him both the doctor and the vet.

I hear him say, "She'll be fine," as he stares down at the offensive and most obtrusive object that has the name of *thermometer*. He runs the thermometer under the faucet and continues to speak to the nice, decorative man, the man with the drawings on his arms, with whom I have spent the most recent night. I have found this decorative man to be both helpful and kind; he brought to me things that smelled of Amy, he brought to me, like magic, my most favorite Duck.

"She'll be fine," the doctor says again, and nods, and the decorative man, he nods, too. They both turn to look at me, and the decorative man holds on to my haunches again, as if I were a flight risk. To tell you the truth, I had not fully considered that being a flight risk was an option. Had I, who knows? I might have embraced the renegade spirit. I might have indeed. The doctor reaches down for my snout and I try to evade his grasp. He smells of pain. He is too quick for me and he holds my snout firmly in his hands. He smells of suffering! He smells of sorrow! He stares, not into my eyes, but into my nose.

"I'm relieved the discoloration is only lichenoid depigmenting mucositis," he says. I have no idea what those words mean, but the way he says them, I do not think they are too bad. "She won't be in any discomfort, though I doubt the color will return," he says next. He rubs my nose lightly. He smells of sadness, of longing, of wanting to be free! He stops staring at my nose. He lets go of my snout, and he speaks more to the decorative man. "All the other tests were fine though. No lupus, which was the big worry. And everything checked out, so for now, unless other symptoms present themselves, it's just a strange, innocuous loss of pigment."

They tested me for lupus!

"It's good it's nothing worse," says the decorative man.

The doctor looks down at me. I stare back. I am defiant. I am relaying, with every fiber of my being: *Do not touch me again on my snout!*

"It's just a bit funny looking, nothing more," the vet says and makes to pat at my head. I duck. "The only problem I can foresee is that she might not have much of a future in front of the camera."

"Well," says the decorative man, "I'm sure she won't mind about that."

"I'm sure she won't," the vet says, and he smiles at me. I do not look at him. I do not return his gaze. I feel I must pause to reflect on what he just said.

And then! And then I am being carried, through the air! I must be being brought back to Amy! *Yay! Yay!* We will be reunited and oh, no. *Oh, no.* I am being carried, still through the air, but we are going the wrong way. I am being placed back in the kennel, and back into my cage. I am back in my cage. Hello, Duck!

Even though she is not here, it smells in here like Amy. It smells like love, and kibble, and safety, and home, and actually, like longing, too. After last night, I am familiar with what longing smells like. I did not think I would be back here again, but I am. I get into my Sphinx position, the one I think works in a pinch at the dinner table when I am trying to show how well behaved I am. I feel it is an appropriate stance for now. But yet. But yet, the decorative man shuts the door of the kennel and tells me in a soft voice that he will be back soon, and that I will go home soon and that I have nothing to worry about, and I think that was very nice of him to let me know that. But, still. As he crosses the room and goes (as people are so wont to do) to the other side of the door, I lay my head down and I sigh.

Without anything else to contemplate, without Amy, I am free to think about what the vet said, how I was not going to have much of a future in front of a camera. I think he means to say "photography." From what I have overheard, work with cameras, which is the work I have most recently been involved in, is called *photography*.

And there is something in me that feels regret at this, just a touch of remorse. I feel I have given my photography my all, as I try to do with everything. I have put my heart into it, my soul into it, as is my way. I am tempted to sigh. I am tempted to think in the way which I believe I have picked up from people. I am tempted to say, "But, oh. But, oh. Why? I have worked so hard. I have been so good." But I do not say that. It occurs to me, in the nick of time, that it is not the photography that has been important. No. I know in my heart, as I lift my head, to rest my chin lightly on the top of Duck, that what has been most important, what has always been most important, is that I gave it my best; what has been most important is that I have always given everything my best.

I feel that it is okay if I do not have a future in front of the cameras. I feel that it is just fine. Even if I will not have a future with photography, I can think of a great many things that I put my heart, my soul, into. I can list a great many things I will have a great future with:

For starters, running.

Creative projects, of course.

Adventure.

Loyalty.

Companionship.

Cheese.

And that is just the beginning. That is just off the top of my head. The possibilities I think, really they are endless.

I look through the cold bars of my kennel with both hope and optimism, in the firm belief that I will see Amy again. Next. It will be the very next thing that will happen. I can feel it. I will see her.

The door opens, and the man with the drawings on his arms reaches in to me. As he does, I am at the same time both quick and careful as I take Duck by the neck in my teeth. The decorative man takes me, and Duck, and he reaches out and grabs the shirt and the shorts that are Amy's, too. I feel that there is kindness in the fact that he does that. I would like a snack. He carries us all to the door and to the other side of it. And there, there, on the other side of the door, as she does seem to sometimes like to be, there, across the room, at last, is Amy.

She is speaking with the doctor, the vet, and yet, I hear her call him something else, something different. She doesn't call him the vet, or the doctor, like everyone else has called him; she calls him "August."

"Thank you," I hear her say, and then I hear her say it again, "August." August. She has not yet seen me on my approach, and there is something in her eyes, in the way she looks, the way she looks at him, that causes me some, if not a lot of, concern. But then Amy, she spies

Alison Pace

me at last, out of the corner of her eye, and her voice changes. It becomes a higher-pitched and louder variation on the nice voice, the soft voice, the voice she uses before bed, when she lets me know that another day has come to an end. In that voice, she says, "Carlie!" and I realize that this day, or however long it has been that I have been here, has at last come to an end, too. And the decorative man, he puts me down, and Amy bends all the way down, and I run the very few steps to her—I run! I run!—and I get so excited that I pee on the floor.

The doctor, the vet, this August, he reaches out to pat my head again, and I duck it. The way that Amy looks at him makes me think she likes him. I do not understand. I look again to her, to be sure. Yes, it's there, in her eyes. She likes him. I do not know why. Can't she see the sorrow, the suffering? Even though his cause may be noble, even though his demeanor may seem kind, doesn't she mind about the pain?

The decorative man pets me, and I let him, but then I turn from him. I am not one to linger on good-byes. Amy and I turn together to the door. This door is one of the wonderful doors. It is the kind that lets you see right through it, all the way clear to the other side. Amy and I go through it. We go through it together. I am leaving with Amy, and in true Westie fashion I will not look behind me. In the true way of the West Highland White Terrier, I will not look back.

26

(amy)

All I Ever Wanted

Carlie and I walk together back into the apartment that no longer seems empty and dark, even if it is still quite small, even if so many of the windows are facing a brick wall.

As soon as I've taken off her harness, I pour Gatorade—red Gatorade, of course—into Carlie's dish. I place it carefully down for her in the living room. If she's thirsty, I don't want her to have to go to the trouble of walking the five to six extra steps to the kitchen. I've wrapped her omega-3 and omega-6 tablets in an envelope of cream cheese and given it to her. August said that it probably would not lessen the effects of the lichenoid depigmenting mucositis, but it might prevent it from getting any worse. Just to have her home, just to have her healthy, and just to have her with me, I wouldn't care, not in the least, if her nose turned a shade of iridescent green. As long as it was, like this is, innocuous. *Innocuous*: perhaps my new favorite word.

Once Carlie has finished her cream cheese and is resting comfortably on the couch, I head briefly to my desk, to my laptop, to turn on music. As New Order begins to pipe rhythmically into my living room, I quickly flip the laptop shut. I don't want to think of that right now. I don't want to be in the eighties right now. And as I sit back down, I make a mental note to navigate my iTunes away from that particular iMix.

I sit back down next to Carlie and try, no matter how difficult a task it may turn out to be, to gather my thoughts. *So, right,* I think, *new development. So, right,* I think, *August.* There is a part of me, I must admit, that wonders if this is just perfect, if this is exactly how everything should be. There's a part of me that wonders if it's just perfect that a woman such as myself, who is a bit obsessed with her dog, whose life has quite literally been built around her dog, should wind up with a vet, a person whose life is built around and dedicated to not only one dog, but to all dogs. It does all seem like the perfectly scripted ending. Though I have begun to wonder if it's wrong to count on a perfectly scripted ending. If nothing else, maybe cable TV has shown me that.

And while I'm here, while I'm on the subject of August, there's something else. There's a thought that keeps popping into my head. No matter how many times I try to push it out, it returns. It is relentless. I keep thinking it. As much as I don't want to, I seem to keep considering that maybe there was something untoward about August's taking me out for a drink in the middle of Carlie's illness. I wonder if there isn't a bit of the unseemly, a bit of the predatory, in the way it all happened, if maybe August shouldn't be involved with his patients, or rather, his patients' people that way. I wonder, and I do hope it's possible to wonder this without seeming ungrateful, without seeming unappreciative for everything that August has done for Carlie.

I lean over toward Carlie and I pet her. I try not to succumb to the nagging, perpetually returning thoughts. Carlie is well and I know that's not really the only thing in the world that matters, but it seems right now that it is.

Carlie, ever the independent, jumps off the couch and heads over to her zebra-striped bed, and I watch her as she settles in. Carlie, who was not rushed into emergency surgery to remove an obstruction as I had feared she would be. Carlie, whose every test has come back okay, is to me like a sign from I don't even know where that things can work out. I look at her there in her zebra-striped bed, the one I bought thinking it would be ironic and whimsical, but now at times I do wonder if the irony, along with the whimsy, is lost.

"Carlie!" I say to her, really for no reason at all. She

gets up from her bed, as her ears point backward and lie back against the top of her head so it looks as if an invisible kerchief has been placed there. As her tail goes down from its alert, upright position and wags quickly, back and forth, between her two hind legs, it seems that everything else is moot. As I say to her, "Ah, the low tail wag," I can't question anything about August's motives. I actually wonder if maybe I'll fall in love with August just because something he did, some care he provided, has made it so this moment exists.

The instructions from the vet office are right there on the coffee table, though they don't need to be, I've already memorized them. Since they say it's a good thing for Carlie to get out and have a stroll, since the walls at this moment feel like maybe they're closing in on me, I decide now is as good a time as any to take Carlie out for said stroll.

As I harness Carlie up and leash her, my eyes fall on her turquoise bandana, lying somewhat forgotten in the corner, as forgotten as the Snake River and *Swim, Carlie, Swim!* has been lately. I grab it from its spot and tie it loosely around her neck. I want to believe it's a positive omen, an arbiter of good things to come. Though I take care to remind myself that now, in the midst of all the new developments, I should not use *Swim, Carlie, Swim!* as an excuse to think too much about Robert Maguire.

Carlie and I head slowly down the stairs and out onto Fifth Street. We head over to Second Avenue and walk down it. Just as we turn onto Fourth Street, and head west again, Carlie pauses for a minute and looks up at me. I smile down at her; I think the turquoise bandana provides a fine counterbalance, a good distraction from the pink- and black-spotted nose. As I look down at her, it occurs to me—remarkably it hasn't already—that Carlie could in fact be concerned over the state of her nose, that is if she is even aware of it. I am, of course, inclined to say she is. I want to be sure she knows there is nothing at all to worry about.

"You look so pretty," I tell her, as we walk slowly down Fourth Street. She looks up at me with what I am sure is a smile. "So pretty," I repeat, and her tail goes low and fast behind her. I bend down beside her and she jumps up into her High Five to Carlie position, balancing on her hind legs, her front paws coming down to meet my shoulders, as she leans in for a kiss.

"So pretty," I say *again*, my hand on the top of her head, because if I say anything else, I just might be at risk for bursting into tears, *again*, down here at dog level to the rest of the world.

"It doesn't work." It comes from above me, because right now, everything is above me. I look up, and I see an older woman, much older, I want to say well into her eighties, though that might be stretching it. I don't stand up, but rather I stay there with Carlie, and from my dog-level vantage point I take in her orange socks, her slippers, the kind of slipper I would say generally shouldn't be worn outside the house. She's wearing a summery skirt, ankle length and bubble-gum pink, and I wonder if she's cold. She has a walker. I look up at her bright pink lips, bubble-gummy, too, and outlined haphazardly with what I think might be black eyeliner. I wonder if maybe she might be insane, if she's recently escaped from Bellevue. But then you wouldn't really think of her as someone who might be able to escape from anywhere, and I wonder if she needs help. There's something about the way she looks at me, independent and proud, that makes me think it would be wrong to ask her if she needs help. I look only briefly into her clear eyes. I focus instead on the heavily mascaraed lashes that surround them, and I say nothing. I smile at her blandly and turn my attention back to Carlie, who switches seamlessly from staring seriously up at the woman along with me, to Renfield.

"Yes," I say to Carlie, trying to focus everything on her, everything other than the part of me that is hoping this strange and unsettling woman will just walk away.

"It doesn't work," the woman says again, still there.

I look up at her again. "What doesn't work?" I ask her, going against my natural inclinations and my better judgment, both of which lean toward not talking to anyone unless absolutely pressed.

"Loving them. Instead of people. It doesn't work."

I don't look away from her, but I don't say anything. I think that's such a terrible thing to say. I stand up to my full height. She looks the same. She looks, standing there, completely fragile and bizarre and old. I look down at her fingers, holding on to her walker, and I think that maybe she looks like she might know that of which she speaks. I can't say anything to her, I know that. I can't ask her why she said that. I'm sure I don't want to know. I pull on Carlie's leash gently, and Carlie snaps to attention. I don't know what to do. I just stand there. The woman takes a step, and then another, pushing her walker out in front of her, her movements much less labored than I would have thought they would have been. I stand there with Carlie for a long time. Until the old woman has turned a corner and I can't see her anymore. I try not to think of what she just said to me, and I tell myself that even if I do, I don't have to think that there is any truth to it.

Instead of continuing on Fourth to Third, Carlie and I turn back and head toward Second. I count in my head *four, three, two, one.* I think of countdowns, I think I'm almost at the end of mine, and I have no idea what happens once I get down to zero.

27

(amy)

Oh, l'Amour

I t's nice to see you," August says, as he walks into my apartment.

"It's nice to see you, too," I say, as Carlie makes a beeline for the fireplace. "Can I get you anything?" I ask. "Something to drink? A beer?" I offer. I do not generally have beer in my apartment; I'm not actually much of a beer drinker. I went out and bought it once August and I made our plan for tonight, and he very nicely said, "I'll come and pick you up."

"No, thanks, though," August says, "I'm all set." There's something very dashing about him. But I try not to think too much about the dashing, because I know where that could go, and I really don't want tonight to be about Robert Maguire.

"Okay, then," I say, "I just have to give Carlie her pills,

and then I'm ready to go." He smiles. I smile. I head into the kitchen. I hide Carlie's pills in a glob of cream cheese, and call for her. I stick my head out into the living room where Carlie is stalking around laboriously, looking both the huntress and the hunted. She sees me and takes a break to come into the kitchen and take the offered cream cheese from me. Immediately, she goes quickly back to her stalking, never taking her suspicious eyes off August. Just as I'm returning the tub of cream cheese to the refrigerator, I notice the invitation on the refrigerator door.

There it is, held in place by a magnet, and it seems like such a long time ago that I first pinned it there. It's an invitation to a party Nick's network is having for *I Really Liked the Eighties a Lot.* It's at Pravda. When I first got the invitation, I remember thinking that Pravda was a place that made people think of the nineties, much more so than the eighties. And yes, once I thought that, I did also think that once a person starts equating bars with decades, it's entirely possible she has been in the same place for too long. But regardless, they should have had the party somewhere that made sense, like Limelight, somewhere that actually existed in the eighties. It bothered me, annoyed me. Even now, I have to remind myself that this is not my party; the location and its lack of irony is not my concern. I move the magnet just slightly, and I see the date. Tonight. *Oh,* I think, *no.*

The last few days have been such a whirlwind, what with the dramatic falling ill of Carlie, that I completely forgot. It's been a bit of a blur. Other than making the date with August, the only thing I can remember doing is calling Renee to request that she tell *them* that Carlie would be out on sick leave, that she explain about the discoloration of Carlie's nose, and to point out that it might be time to take another look at the contracts. And, also, I spoke briefly to Bonnie, who was nice enough to call to check on Carlie's health. In the last few days, I haven't actually thought of Nick. The music has been momentarily turned off. Suddenly, a wave of images sweeps over me: his eyes, his hair, his hands. I wonder if it's possible to miss someone you don't even know that well.

I think I have to go to his party. I should go if for no other reason than Nick came to my party, even if everything there went so wrong so quickly. What even happened? I don't even know. I have August in my living room. I can't kick him out in order to go to the party. And yet I feel I can't not go. What choice do I have?

I take the magnet from the refrigerator in one hand, and take the invitation in the other. As I pop my head out into the living room, I can't help thinking, *Look at me with technically (very technically) two men in my life*. And not even one of them is Jonathan, and not even one of them is fictional.

August is standing directly in front of my coffee table,

hands thrust deeply into his khakis, his jaw slack, his face a bit blank. He seems to be focused on an empty spot on the wall. Carlie, by the way, is nowhere to be seen.

"August?" I say.

"Amy," he says, shaking his head quickly, once to the left and once to the right, focusing his eyes, as if I've just woken him from a nap. "Yes."

I smile back at him, just a bit weakly, and walk the short distance to where he stands. I hold the invitation out to him, thinking this may be a conversation that could be helped by the use of visual aids. I reach out with my last steps, stiff cardboard party invitation in my outstretched hand. For an instant there, August and I are two choreographed and practiced members of a water ballet, as he reaches out gracefully and takes the invitation from my hand. He looks down at it, with only the slightest wrinkling of his brow. And really, I tell myself, that could just be concentration. There should be no reason at all why I feel apprehensive asking August if he'd like to go to Nick's party. This is what I tell myself. *Right, yes,* I think to myself, it's not about Nick, per se. It's about Nick's party, simply an event to which I will take August, to meet people I know, to be out in the world and see things. I can't help but wonder who it is I am trying to fool, as if going out to a party, to see people, to be out and about, is an activity I would ever willingly think of as something I might like to do.

August is looking at me, waiting.

"This is for a party for a coworker of mine," I begin. "Well, technically he's not a coworker, but his show tapes right next to Carlie's show, and I sort of forgot it was tonight?" I begin. "And he came to the party for Carlie's first show, so I should kind of go to this," I add on a bit lamely, as if my party had been a party somewhere, as if it hadn't been tea sandwiches in my apartment. I wonder if that night, and everything that happened, might have turned out differently if it had been held somewhere else. I suspect not. I suspect location was not among my many problems.

August is looking at me, waiting.

"And I was hoping you wouldn't mind going with me tonight?"

"Oh," he says, looking only very briefly flustered, and I think maybe slightly disappointed, but that could just be me projecting. "Okay, sure." He nods at me in agreement. Even though I have the uncomfortable sensation of inner conflict growing in my stomach, I smile back at him, and I nod, too. Then Carlie appears as if out of nowhere to look at me expectantly, or is that accusingly?

* * *

The first thing I notice, once we've taxied the short distance over to Lafayette Street and walked into Pravda, is the glitter. There is glitter everywhere. It seems to be falling down like rain from the ceiling and I wonder if I'm covered in it, if everyone is. I stretch out my arms in front of me to see if they're covered, but with all the flashing lights, it's too hard to tell. The second thing I notice is that everyone is in costume, dressed up mostly as various characters from the eighties. I see a few Reagan masks, several Madonnas, and a tremendous amount of fluorescent hair. I forgot about the costume part of the night. I have no idea what I would have dressed as if I'd paid attention. As August and I inch closer into the room, the song "Runaway Train" starts playing through the speakers and I think that's somehow wrong.

"That song?" I say, turning to August. "That song is definitely not from the eighties. It's from the nineties. I mean, early nineties, say ninety-two, ninety-three, I'm not sure, but still they're very different time periods."

August looks at me a bit blankly, no, make that completely blankly, and then he puts a hand up to his ear, cupping it in a way that I would have to say was dramatically.

"What's that?" he says, perhaps a bit louder than necessary. "I can't really hear you."

"It just doesn't really make a tremendous amount of sense, to play a nineties song at a party for a show about eighties music?" I say loudly. "It can just get so frustrating, it can just leave you with that feeling of, what's the point of it all anyway. I mean, I know that in the scheme of things, 'what's the point' probably wouldn't make a list of top ten bad feelings, but still, it can be upsetting."

August looks at me blankly. He shakes his head no. I'm aware on some level that this is, technically, our first official date, and this is neither the best venue nor conversation for our technical first date. August holds both his hands out, palms up, and shakes his head quickly, the universally accepted motion for "Honey, I've got no idea what you're talking about." It occurs to me that maybe neither do I. As I look out at the room, as whatever infuriatingly non-eighties band whose name I don't even know is going on about runaway trains, never coming back, and going the wrong way on a one-way track, I get this feeling that everything about this song is wrong, except for maybe the lyrics.

It's only a minute or so later that Echo and the Bunnymen, a band I know I'm only able to identify because of Nick, starts piping through the speakers. A song called "Bring on the Dancing Horses" begins playing and for the briefest of brief milliseconds, I wonder if everything is right with the world.

I smile back at August. Maybe he really can't hear me, maybe it's not his fault. Maybe no one can hear anyone else over the music. Maybe when I look back on this period of my life, that will turn out to have been my prevailing problem. No one could hear me over the music, and I couldn't hear anyone either.

August and I are standing side by side, listening to the music. All this time I've thought of listening to old music as living in the past, but maybe it's not, maybe there's something about it that's living in the present.

I look over at August, and I notice his eyes, scanning the room. I begin a quick scan myself, but I don't get very far, because almost immediately my gaze falls on Nick. Over by the foot of the stairs, across a field of glitter, there's Nick. As a flash from a strobe light passes in front of his face, I think he looks pale. A cluster of people that was partially obscuring him from view moves and I see his entire length stretched out, forming a tilted cross with the banister. I look away from Nick and over at August. August, I remind myself, who's a vet, and who saved my dog, and who could be perfect. Except that I don't want to believe in perfect anymore. Except I don't want to want perfect anymore. My head hurts. I turn to August.

"Um, over there," I say, indicating the staircase, "is the man whose party this is, whose show this is a party for. Do you mind if I go over and say hi? I'll be right back?" August smiles at me and nods agreeably. And then he starts to walk across the room with me.

As we cross the floor and walk through the glitter, a streamer sticks ever so briefly to my forehead and then is gone. We get closer and soon enough, we're right in front of Nick. I can read the white letters across his

T-shirt. *Oh, l'Amour,* it says. *Oh, love,* it's impossible not to think.

"Hi, Nick," I say cautiously. My head is beginning to pound.

"Hi, Amy," he says, and I have to wonder if the way in which he says it is maybe a little standoffish.

"Nick," I say, "this is August. August, this is Nick." I gesture between them with my hand. They shake hands.

There is a silence, one that could indeed be categorized as awkward; I am compelled, as I imagine people are in these situations, to fill it.

"So," I say to Nick, for lack of anything else to say, "I guess you didn't dress up either?" I have the idea suddenly that maybe that's why costume parties were invented, so that people could have something to say to each other. Nick looks at me; I might even say he looks hard at me. In his eyes I think I see, along with the general background sadness, disappointment. I wish I could think it's just because I may have in some way just insulted his costume efforts.

"I'm Vince Clarke," he says.

"I don't get it," I say. I have no idea why I thought this was a good thing to say next.

"No," he says, in a different sort of tone than the one he used before, this one almost imperceptibly softer, "I don't think you do."

I want to tell Nick that I thought I did; that I thought I got it. But I don't think that will make any sense, and so I don't say anything at all. Nick doesn't say anything else. I wonder if that's because there isn't anything left to say. Nick turns away from me, and faces August.

"It was nice to meet you," he says to August, and then adds on a vague, "thanks for coming," that I imagine to be directed to both of us. As he walks away, I remember Nick telling me as we walked through the streets of the East Village that Vince Clarke was at one time or another a key member of Depeche Mode, Yaz, and Erasure. *I messed up,* I think. I messed up. And it has nothing at all to do with not knowing who Vince Clarke was just now.

"Amy! Hi! I'm so happy to see you here!" August and I turn simultaneously to see Bonnie approaching, a taller and thinner and prettier version of Madonna.

"Bonnie, hi," I say, admiring the number of black rubber bracelets that cover half her forearm, "it's great to see you. Bonnie," I continue, gesturing to August, "this is August. August, this is Bonnie." They stare at each other for a moment with sparkly eyes. I smile. They continue to stare. I feel any guilt over dragging August to this party, over not being as nice as I could have been to Bonnie originally, melt away. *Bonnie and August,* I think. They're still staring. And even with Nick, and his walking quickly away, and even with all the things I may have messed up, I don't feel jealous at all. I think that maybe Bonnie and August could be a really good thing. Strangely, as soon as I think that, any worries I had about August being a predatory sort, they fade away, too.

August stares dreamily, transfixed with Bonnie. Bonnie, with a toss of her crimped hair, says she was just on her way to the bar to get a drink.

"Oh, allow me," says August. "Amy, can I get you something, too?"

"No, I'm fine," I say. "And August?"

He pulls his gaze away from Bonnie's exposed midriff, and looks over at me. "Yes?"

"Thanks," I say. "Thanks for everything."

"Of course," he says looking at me a bit bemusedly, but maybe a bit like he understands exactly what I'm saying, too. And then he's off, heading zealously to the bar.

The moment he's a few steps away, Bonnie turns to me with wide and curious eyes. "Who's that?" she asks.

"He's Carlie's vet," I say.

"Oh, really, oh, wow," she says. "Are you and he . . . ?"

"No," I say. "No. Actually I was thinking maybe I saw some sparks between the two of you?" I lead, just to make sure.

"Not if he's here with you. Definitely not if he's here with you," she says. *Nice Bonnie,* I think.

"No, really, just friends," I say, allowing myself the slight technical lie. "I think you should go for it. Go meet him at the bar."

"Cool, Amy," she says giving me a thumbs-up, turning slightly in the direction of the bar.

"Oh, but Bonnie?"

"Yes?"

"Would you mind telling August that I had to go?"

"Oh, sure," she says. "But is everything okay?"

"Yes," I say, even though technically the answer is, *Not yet*. "And Bonnie, thanks to you, too."

She looks at me confused, then she smiles, and then she dashes to the bar.

As I head to the exit, Whitney Houston is playing. I listen to her singing, something about the years that pass us by. The years and years and years. And I think, in this order: work needs to be done, things need to be set straight, and amends need to be made.

28

(amy)

Amy, What You Wanna Do?

The lease renewal for my apartment arrived in yesterday afternoon's mail, a yellow fluorescent highlighter on how much time I've already spent here. Production on *Things to Do in the City with Your Dog* has been on hiatus while Erin and Barton debate the pros and cons of a canine hostess with a gamy-looking nose, while Renee reviews the intricacies of my contract, and while, it would be my guess, a bevy of Brussels Griffons are paraded out to Long Island City where they circle sharklike around Carlie's empty director's chair. I try not to think too much of how relieved I'll be if at the end of this week I'm told it is not only I who have been recast, but also Carlie.

I've been writing. I haven't been writing my novel, but I have been working diligently on *Swim, Carlie, Swim!* I have, for the first time, a good idea of how it's all going to end up.

As a midmorning break, Carlie and I have taken a leisurely stroll over to Union Square, to the Barnes & Noble here. It's been a long time since I've been able to be in a bookstore without feeling jealousy. But today, as I've been so recently productive, today as I can almost see an ending that I might actually like, the bookstore is, again, just a nice place to be.

Once Carlie and I have visited the children's section to see the three existing *Run, Carlie, Run!* books still displayed on the shelves, and once I've managed to make it through the new-fiction section without feeling venomous, once I've enjoyed the bookstore in the way that I used to, in the way that might be a little bit hopeful, we head back out to Union Square.

As we step out onto the sidewalk, the late October air is crisp and brisk. The days are getting shorter, but they're also getting somehow fresher, less bogged down by the heat of the city in which they unfold. There's something about fall in New York, the way it sneaks up on you, even though you've spent the better part of a seemingly endless August (the month, not the vet) waiting for it. Fall days in New York, like this one, are the good days. They're the days that can make you see there is so much in this city, so much that is vibrant and alive and exciting and exhilarating, even though what comes with that is a little bit dirty and crowded and perhaps for some, just the slightest bit soul-destroying.

Good fall days like this one are the types of days that make you appreciate New York, that make you see all the good in it, even if you haven't had the recent benefit of following your canine around the city with a film crew in search of such enlightenment. I look across at Union Square, at what can so aptly be described, without any hokiness or misplaced irony, as hustle and bustle. I look down either side, at the vendors, the traffic jams, the restaurants, the stores, the bank building that's now a theatre. I look at the city in front of me, all around me, the city I think I've been in so long now that no matter how far away I may go from it, it will always be a part of me.

As I turn with Carlie, suddenly I see Lara, wandering aimlessly in front of Sephora. She's clutching her gigantic bright-blue Goyard bag to her chest, looking around anxiously, like a confused rabbit only just recently released from its warren. It's strange to see her down here, so out of context, as if a puppet from a puppet theatre had escaped her puppet stage and was out, running around, loose on the street.

There's a part of me, quite a big part of me, that doesn't want to, but I walk over to her. I reach out and touch her shoulder. "Lara?" I say.

She flails around quickly with a sharp intake of breath, her long straight hair almost hitting me in the face as it whips around. When she sees that it's me, her expression softens and her posture relaxes a bit. "Oh, Amy!" she says, reaching out to grab my wrist, while still managing to keep her bag secure at her breast. "Thank God it's you!"

"Is everything okay?" I ask. Carlie stares up at her intently. I wonder if Carlie is not particularly fond of Lara, or if I am, not for the first time, only projecting my own inner thoughts onto Carlie.

"Yes, yes," she says, still looking around a bit nervously. "Guillermo?" she says next.

"What's that?" I say, at a loss.

"Guillermo," she repeats, kind of impatiently. "My hairdresser?"

"Oh," I say, "right, right. Guillermo," as if the mentioning of Guillermo clears things up, as if Guillermo is not completely apropos of nothing at all.

"Right," she continues, relaxing visibly in front of me, as exasperation seems to take over. "He left Frederic Fekkai, if you can believe it? I mean, really."

I nod with something just short of comprehension.

"And he came down here to some place called Butterfly Salon, and I can't find it."

"What's the address?" I ask her. "I can help you find it."

"No," she says, "no. I'm too flustered. I'm too annoyed now. I don't want to get my hair cut when I'm annoyed.

It's bad karma. And I think it'd just be better if I went to someone new at Fekkai, really, rather than having to come all the way down here every time I need a haircut. It's too much of a nightmare. How do you *live here?*" she asks me. When I don't answer, she changes tack and says, "Well, now that I *am* here and all, do you want to get lunch? It's been a long time. I called you, you know," she adds on, just the slightest bit accusingly.

It has been a long time, I think, and I reach into my bag to take a quick look at my cell phone. I glance at the digital time display, and toss the cell phone back in. "Yes," I say, "that'd be nice. It's eleven thirty, so if you don't mind sitting outside we could just go to Coffee Shop, over there," I say, pointing to the opposite corner and one block down.

"Why do we have to sit outside?" she asks.

"Because of Carlie," I say.

Lara looks down. "Oh," she says. "Hi, Carlie."

As we cross the street, Lara turns to me and asks, "Do they have a nice brunch there?" I imagine Lara picturing Sarabeth's, either at the Whitney Museum or the one farther up Madison Avenue on Ninety-fourth Street; I imagine her picturing the fresh-baked muffins, the charming tureens of handmade jam. I stop walking for just a step and turn to face her.

"No," I tell her.

Once we've been seated and ordered, and our salads

have arrived and I have both refrained from drinking before noon and marveled that no information on Jonathan's destination wedding or the fact that his fiancée is actually having trust-fund triplets is forthcoming, Lara looks up and asks me, quite completely out of nowhere. "So, any men?"

I look up, surprised by the question, and then, even more so by my answer. "Yes, sort of," I say. Lara looks up and places down her fork, waiting, it appears, for more information. "His name is Nick," I say, and really, I don't even think I knew I was going to say his name. It's not as if I were going to say anyone else's name, I'm just not sure Nick can count as a man in my life. I wonder how it's possible to feel like you've lost someone when maybe you never even found him. But then there is a part of me that feels as if he's been here all along, and as if it somehow makes sense that I just said his name.

"Where's he from?" Lara asks.

"He's from here," I say. "He lives in Stuyvesant Town."

"Did he move there before or after it went co-op?" she asks, and I ignore the question. I pick a piece of bacon out of my Cobb salad and sneak it down to Carlie. I think maybe Lara has just rolled her eyes.

"What does he do?" she inquires.

"He's a scholar of eighties music," I say. This time when she rolls her eyes, I'm sure of it.

"Lara, what?" I demand.

"Amy, don't get defensive, but just, is this realistic? I mean what are you going to do? Live on love alone?"

"No," I say.

"Listen," she says back. "Don't look like that, and I'm sure this Nick is a very nice person, all I meant was, I think after everything you've been through already, normal is what you want."

"No," I say, "it's not."

"Amy. After everything," she says next, stressing the *everything* to a point that I really am tempted to correct her, to say it wasn't *that* much, "I think you should want someone who can take care of you."

"Lara," I say calmly as I signal for the check, "I can take care of myself."

"Suit yourself," Lara says after a pause. Then she busies herself with arranging her Goyard bag so that the hand-painted initials and the red and green colors she has selected for the racing stripe are facing out, lest anyone mistake it for a fraud.

*   *   *

Once Carlie and I are back outside, once Lara has hastily hailed a cab even though it was heading the wrong way down Broadway, I don't make it all the way across Union Square toward points east. I stop in the middle of the small slice of green that passes for a park, and I look around again. I turn slowly around and look at the circular view as I go. I look up at the restaurants and stores, and all the words written on them spin in front of my eyes and through my head. I look around the perimeter, at the buildings, at the slogans everywhere, words, and names, and that building on Broadway with the numbers ticking away to who even knows what, the smoke pouring out of it as if there weren't already enough random occurrences of mysterious smoke in New York.

I moved here, I think, *I chose this.* I am the only person I can hold responsible for my choices. It made so much sense at the time, it did. I wanted to be downtown, to be vital, to be part of the creativity that I'd always heard was here. I wanted to be part of it. I think that was mostly because I thought it would help me to do my own work. It seemed like such a good idea at the time.

But now, standing in the middle of all these buildings and words and people, everywhere I look, buildings and words and people, all I can think about is mountains, and rivers, and sky. All I can think about is a place that's so different from here. I want mountains and rivers and sky and trees. I want three hundred and twelve days of sun a year, and 25 percent humidity every day. After all these years of looking out the window and seeing a brick wall and, sometimes, dead pigeons, I want to look out the window and see the Front Range. I want to be in a place of beauty, real beauty, natural beauty. This, I'm sure of it, is what I want. All I can think about is home.

Every book I've ever written is about leaving New York. "Maybe that's something you should explore," Renee had told me once. "Maybe it is," is what I'd said then.

I walk across Park Avenue South, hurrying Carlie along. She wants to stop every few inches to sniff things, and I feel as if I can't get back quickly enough. Somehow, soon enough, we're back on Fifth Street, we're at our door. I hurry up the stairs, and once we're inside, I give the ever-flexible and agreeable Carlie a biscuit, and then a saltine cracker for good measure.

I sit down at my laptop. I know what to do.

29

(robert maguire)

Walk Away, Renee

I would very much like to be able to say to you now that I don't actually have any idea why I'm here. Only, I do. I have good reason to believe this meeting is about me.

Amy has walked up to Irving Place, to a café here named quite appropriately, 71 Irving Place. There is a lot of tile here, and old wooden chairs and tables. It's very crowded. Everywhere, there are people hunched over their laptop computers. Amy walks up to the counter and orders a cappuccino. She asks for it in a to-go cup, even though I know she has every intention of staying here for a while. But yet, I hold on to the hope that she may just decide to leave after all. She may just decide that none of this needs to happen after all.

She carries her cappuccino with her, through the sea of people, to a small table up in the front of the café, right by the window. I am now powerless to do anything but watch as Renee walks into the café and joins her. I have at this point lost so much of my influence. I do wonder if it is because I did quite undeniably abuse my power. Renee signals for a waitress as she sits down, even though there is no waitress service here.

"I think you have to go up to the bar for service," Amy explains. Renee eyes the offending line at the bar, several people deep.

"Oh, then," Renee says, her eyes falling briefly on Amy's beverage, "I'm okay then. What's up? On the phone, you sounded like it was urgent?"

"Thanks for meeting me on such short notice," Amy says, as she reaches down into her bag. She removes a manila folder filled with paper, and a compact disc, and hands them both proudly across the table to Renee.

"What's this?" Renee says taking the items in her hands, and then, with brightened eyes, looking up at Amy. "Is it . . . ?"

"Yes," Amy says. "*Swim, Carlie, Swim!: Carlie on the Snake River.*"

"Amy, this is terrific," Renee says happily. "Congratulations, I know how hard this was for you." She reaches both her arms across the table. *Oh, yay,* I think, with deepest sarcasm, *Group Hug.*

"Renee, there's more," Amy has to add. *Amy, no.*

"More?" Renee inquires. She sits up straighter in her

chair. Renee can hear, as I can hear, that the *more* is not a good *more*. She can hear, as I can, that Amy's next sentence is not going to be about plans she has made for my and Carlie's return trip to Kinshasa as we had such a fine time whilst last there. That's not what she's going to say. I already know. I already know what she's going to say next.

"Renee," she says. "This is the last of the Carlie books. In it, Robert Maguire gets married to a river guide named Wendy."

Renee looks up, eyes wide, mouth open. She cannot speak. She is at once at a loss for words. I understand exactly how she feels. Amy continues.

"Wendy and Robert Maguire and Carlie are going to settle down and live together in Wyoming," she explains. And, oh! I can't bear it! I truly cannot! A lifetime in wildest Wyoming looking after the wee beast! Does no one care what I want? Does no one care how fond I have grown, in recent months, of New York?

"What?" Renee manages at last.

"This is the last *Run, Carlie, Run!* book," Amy repeats, quite happily. "Robert Maguire is married off, and they're all going to live happily ever after. Her name is Wendy." *Oh, Wendy, Wendy, Wendy. Stop saying Wendy.* I wish she would stop saying *Wendy*.

"Amy, I mean, just think about it," Renee says. There is, in her tone, the usual expected urgency. In addition to the urgency, just underneath it, I hear something that

I've never heard before from Renee: resignation. "Amy," she implores. "Marriage doesn't have to be the end."

"No, I know that," Amy says, and she pauses for a minute, looks down at her hands, and smiles. "Believe me, I know that."

"I mean," Renee continues, "Harry Potter went to seven," she says softly, as softly as she has ever said anything. "Carlie could have gone to eight, no problem. Probably even to ten."

"I'm sorry, Renee," Amy says, "but I'm done. I think this is the best ending for everyone." *Dear God, no.*

Renee stares blankly out the window for a moment and then she shakes her head, almost imperceptibly, and says softly, almost robotically, "I think you're making a mistake, but if it's what you want, I support you."

"Thank you, Renee," Amy says. "And, also, how's it coming with the TV contract?"

"Right, right," Renee says, absentmindedly, distractedly. "The illness clause is there. If you want an out, you have it."

"That's good," Amy says, "I'm going to take it. Thanks."

"Uh-huh," Renee says. That is all she says. To tell you the truth, I was wishing, I was hoping that she was going to do something. Renee of all people, she really could have done something. I had always thought Renee to be among my biggest fans.

As the brief and distressing meeting comes to an end, I feel myself quite literally slipping away, powerless to delay the end. Renee leans across the table and gives Amy a quick peck on the cheek. As Renee turns to leave, I catch something in her eye, a glimmer, the beginnings of a look, that lets me know there is a part of her that doesn't accept that it's really over. I understand. I don't accept it either. I watch Renee for one more moment, as she walks through the door with her head held high, her chin leading the way.

Don't worry too much about Renee. She is, at this moment, disappointed, maybe even saddened, but she won't stay down for long. Renee, I've come to see, is of the sort that will always bounce back, will always carry on, continue, survive. She's looking ahead; she's thinking of the next manuscript to land on her desk. She's thinking of where it might lead her. She's thinking of where she might lead it. She's sure that somewhere out there lies the next big thing. She knows it's somewhere, waiting to be found. She knows she's the one to find it. She knows in her heart that for her it is a matter of perseverance, it always has been.

And me, alas. I imagine I should say don't worry too much about me either. I imagine I should say I've heard Wyoming can be quite nice this time of year. I'd like to believe that maybe it really is. And I'd like to believe also that maybe, in the way of writers everywhere, Amy has put quite a bit of herself into the character of Wendy. That, I think, would work out well. That, I think, would in fact be lovely. Because I'm sure you know that for all this time that Amy has thought about me, waited for me, hoped for me, and maybe even loved me, I have not sat idly by. I am sure you know that I have loved her, too.

30

(amy)

I Think I Could Stay with You

I leave 71 Irving Place, and I head to the subway. I need to go out to Long Island City. I'm aware that it might seem a bit odd. I'm aware that it might seem that the last thing I'd want to do right now, upon the occasion of my freedom, would be to head right back to the scene of the crimes, or at least to the scene of *Things to Do in the City with Your Dog*. And it is. But Long Island City, and the studio there, is also where Nick is. At least it's where I hope I'll find him.

* * *

The first thing I hear upon my arrival at the studio is, "The elevator's down, ma'am."

"Sorry?" I say, just to be sure.

"Elevator's down," I am told again by this man I've

never seen before. I don't know what his job is other than to tell people that the elevator is broken. He points in the direction of the stairwell.

"Thank you," I say, and as I head for the same stairs I ran down with Carlie not very long ago at all, I think to myself that it's only two flights. Even if each flight is about twenty feet high. As I walk into the stairwell and start up the stairs, I don't want to walk slowly. I don't want to delay. I don't want this all to take any longer than it already has. I start to take the steps two at a time, spurred on by a bit of adrenaline, and by something else, too; maybe it's hope. As I travel upward, propelled to my destination, I am for a moment the heroine of every romantic story ever told. I am running through every rain-slicked street in every city on earth. I am pushing my way through every crowd assembled. I am racing through every airport in the world. I am climbing every high mountain. I am swimming across every deepest sea.

I reach Nick's office. I reach up and I knock on Nick's door.

"Come in," he says. I turn the handle. There is, of course, music playing. I listen closer. I think I've heard this song before. I think it's the Pet Shop Boys' cover of "Always on My Mind," and I'm not even surprised I know that. There was a time that I didn't. I take a deep breath, and as I walk through the door, Nick looks up.

"Hi," I say.

"Hi," he says.

"I like this song," I say. He smiles at me, and it makes me think, or maybe the right word here is *hope*, that there are still things left to say. And so I keep talking. "It's the kind of song that just makes you want to sing all the words."

"Yes," he says, and smiles, and trust me when I tell you that it's a really nice smile. "But you don't have to do that. Song lyrics can get really expensive," he says and smiles again. "You know, to reprint them all."

"I know," I say.

"Maybe you don't have to say everything," he says. "Maybe just knowing what the gist is, is enough," he tells me, and I think that he's letting me and my former missteps, and mistakes, off the hook.

"Nick," I say, "then I won't say everything, but I just want you to know that I'm sorry for acting a bit, um, sporadically."

"I think *confusingly* might be the word you're looking for," he says.

"I think it might be."

"It's okay," he says.

"Nick?"

"Amy?"

I take a deep breath. "I came here to tell you that I'd like to get to know you. I'd just like to get to know you and I don't think we've had enough time to do that. Yet. I don't know, maybe someday we might be together, we might be really good together. But first, I'd really just like to get to know you," I say.

Nick stands up behind his desk. He walks out from behind it and comes to stand right in front of me. He places one of his hands on my shoulder, and then he places his other hand on my other shoulder. I look up at him. I look at the blue of his eyes, the bluish tint just underneath the surface of his skin, the bluish-black color of his hair. There isn't even a trace of blue eyeliner.

"I'd like that, too, Amy," he says. And I smile and I breathe, and I think, again, *God, I really wish he would kiss me*. And then for a moment the only thing I can think is that I wish I didn't have to go on. But I know that I do.

"Here's the thing though," I say, "it's going to be a little bit harder now."

He raises his eyebrows. "Harder?" he asks.

"Because I'm leaving New York," I say. "I'm moving back home. I'm moving back to Colorado."

"You're from Colorado?" he asks, confused.

"Yes," I say.

"Really? I never asked," he says. "I should have asked. I just always thought of you as a New Yorker." And I can't help thinking, *Well, would you look at that?*

"I've been here a really long time," I say. "I've spent a lot of my time here trying to fit into one part of it or another. I think I've finally figured out that I don't need to fit in. What I need is to go home. I just lost sight for a while of where exactly home was."

He looks at me, letting everything I've said sink in, and I wonder if I've lost him. But something in his eyes, in the way he looks at me, makes me think I haven't lost him, not yet.

"Colorado?" he muses.

"Right near Boulder," I say. "If you ever wanted to, maybe you could visit?"

"I'll visit you," he says instantly. "I'll definitely visit you."

I think of the first time I saw him, how everything about him seemed blue. It wasn't until the second time I saw him that I learned there was a song that explains exactly who he is, only I didn't know it then. *I'm Mr. Blue, and I'm here to stay with you.* I smile up at him. He smiles back at me. He leans down. And then, finally, he kisses me.

*   *   *

Later, much later, once the camera has delicately panned away from the characters and focused for a while on a lampshade, so to speak, Nick and I are sitting in my living room contemplating all the empty boxes I've yet to start packing. Carlie sits between us on the couch, her chin gently resting on Nick's knee. Once we've consulted Nick's shooting schedule and booked him a flight to Denver for exactly three weeks from today, he turns to me and says, "So?"

"Yes?" I say, noticing that he tilts his head in a way that has always put me in mind of Jack Russell terriers.

"I guess you're not worried anymore that if we end up together, we'll never leave the house again?"

I lean back on the couch a bit. "How did you know that?" I ask him.

"I don't know," he says. "It was just this hunch I got."

"Huh," I say. "No, I'm not so worried about that anymore. I like to stay home," I joke. Half joke. He smiles at me. He gets it. He understands in a way that only a person who would be perfectly content not to leave his house for a few days would understand.

"Well," he says.

"Well," I say, and he laughs softly. I smile back at the reflected image I hope I'll always see in his eyes.

"Do you know what we should do about that?" he asks me.

"I don't know," I say. Except that I do. I think that when I look back on everything, when I want to tell someone my story, I won't ever be confused anymore as to how it started or when it started. Because it starts like this. It starts right here. "What do *you* think we should do about it?" I ask him, throwing him a softball, if for no other reason than the man deserves a softball.

Nick raises an eyebrow. The grin that was already there gets just the slightest bit bigger, and there's a flash, a perfectly timed flash in his eye, right before he delivers my punch line.

"I think one day we should live in a really big house," he says, and his grin turns into a smile.

"A really big house?" I say, because I like the way it sounds and I want to hear it again.

"A really big house," he says.

"That," I say, "sounds like an excellent idea."

31

(amy)

Back in the High Life Again

It all happened very quickly. As it turns out, sometimes things do. *Things to Do in the City with Your Dog* now stars a basset hound named Claude. It's been picked up for a second season. For the most part, I try not to watch it, and for the most part I try not to listen to things I might hear about it. But when I do, I hear it's giving *Meerkat Manor* a run for its money. Sometimes I think, well, good for them. But most of the time, I don't. Though I am very happy for Bonnie, who is enjoying the success and is still dating Dr. Tarquin. She tells me things are going well.

Swim, Carlie, Swim!: Carlie on the Snake River came out just about a month ago and it's been on the bestseller lists since then. And while I've gotten quite a few letters from readers, and more than a request or two from my agent to consider sending Carlie and Robert Maguire out on another adventure, I'm going to leave them where they are, and let them enjoy their much-deserved rest. I truly believe that Robert Maguire and the fictional Carlie are very happy in the life I've chosen for them. The life I've chosen for them is a good one. I can say the same thing about the life I've chosen for myself, too.

I did get the big house. And I live in it without a lot of furniture. Notice, if you haven't already, that the pronoun I'm using here is *I*. And sure, yes, believe me, I know all about the safety there is in the unequivocally happy ending. I've spent the entirety of my writing career, nascent though it is, building the unequivocally happy ending. But in that time, while I was doing it, while that's what I was building up to and hoping for and working toward, I don't think I fully understood the strength, the satisfaction, and the peace that can come from working your way out of an ending that's maybe not so happy. I've learned along the way that there's quite a lot to be said for the possibly happy, too.

I live in what I think is the most beautiful place in the world, and I'm working on my novel. It's a new novel now because I scrapped the original idea and started fresh. It was time to start fresh. This one is still in its very early stages but it's coming together, I think. It's a romantic comedy and a mystery set against the backdrop of the board game Clue. I think it's going to work out well.

And Nick? Nick's good. Nick's really wonderful, in fact. Nick doesn't live in Colorado. Not yet. But he makes it out to visit just about every three weeks. He's finishing out the year left on his contract with *I Really Liked the Eighties a Lot,* and even though he's in a rush to leave and I get that, I really do, the good thing is that I get to see him, once a week, on my TV screen, eyeliner and all. And even though it's not the realest thing in the world, it's something. When he's finished with the show, he's going to start work on his own book, his own version of the thing he always wanted to do, a scholarly tome on the music of the eighties. He's already sold the proposal and received a really excellent advance from Argonaut Press. (Tom Gruen will not be editing.) And he may in fact be able to write the book, for the most part, from Colorado. He'll see. We'll see. I'm not in a rush. I'm not a New Yorker anymore.

And, here. It's beautiful here. I live in the foothills of the Rocky Mountains, a few miles outside Boulder. I look out my window every morning, and I see the Front Range. There's an old chicken coop out back, and even though there aren't any chickens in it, it has become among Carlie's favorite places to spend her time.

Carlie spends much of the day perched on a hill, staring at the chicken coop, in a way I am convinced is deliriously happily. Her mouth is open and I like to think her panting is perhaps a contemplation of all her endless possibilities. She seems constantly amazed and in awe of the wide-open spaces, but somehow I feel she always knew this was coming, long before I did. Intermittently, she briefly pauses her vigil for a run.

She turns and she runs. She puts her whole heart, her whole soul, into her running. And when I'm watching her, every now and then, ever so rarely, I catch her stealing a quick glance in my direction. It's only for an instant, but the fact that she's checking on me is unmistakable. It is in these moments, as the wind whisks her fur straight back, as I see the muscles of her little body rippling with exertion and strength and endless joy, as I see the determined look in her eye, that I feel almost certain that if I listened closely enough, I'd be able to hear her say, "Look! Look! Look at me run!"